Christmas in Comets Valley

MEG READING

Edit by My Brother's Editor

Proofread by Roxana Coumans

Illustration and Cover Design by Melody Jeffries Design, www.melodyjeffriesdesign.com

*To everyone who fast forwarded through Iris and Miles' scenes,
so they could swoon over Graham and Amanda.*

1

AERA

I'D COME to learn that people handle breakups in one of two ways. One, it broke their heart and thrust them into a spiraling pit of despair. Or two, it shaped and molded them into a better version of themself.

And ten months after finding out my ex-fiancé, Tye, had been cheating on me for the *entirety* of our decade long relationship, I could confidently say our breakup had simultaneously done both.

To the eyes of the world, I was accomplishing the goals I'd dreamed of since the day Ben and I started our fashion brand, Inamra, eleven years ago. While in reality, I was sitting at home alone, holed up in the darkness of my bedroom. Much like I had been for the past three hundred days since the breakup.

I knew my relationship with Tye hadn't been picture perfect, but then again, whose relationship was? So what if we didn't have sex every day or even every week? Okay, maybe it was more like once a month… if that.

In my defense, we both owned two of the fastest growing companies in the country, so forgive me if it was a little hard to find the time. Between days chock-full of meetings, which were immediately followed by late nights at the office finalizing last-minute projects, sex was the last thing on either of our minds.

Or so I thought until ten months ago when I stepped foot into Tye's office for a surprise lunch date after one of my meetings got canceled and quickly learned I was the only one in our relationship who couldn't find time for sex.

Much to my surprise, when I opened the door to his corner office, I found Tye's secretary bent over his mahogany desk while he jackhammered in and out of her like a madman.

She must've been an out-of-work actress based on how piercing and animated her moans were. She and I both knew he wasn't that good, no matter how hard she tried to convince herself otherwise.

I couldn't help but feel bad for the people in the offices next to him who had to listen to her shrill voice yelling, "Fuck me, daddy." Over and over again.

The two of them were too enamored with their impending orgasms to notice I was standing in the door-way, staring back at them wide eyed with my breath caught in my lungs.

In a fit of rage, I stormed out of the building and left the door wide open, hoping it would ruin the high of their orgasms when they came back to earth and realized one of their coworkers could've stopped by to watch the show.

A quick word to the wise: if you're planning on banging your secretary during your lunch hour, at least have the brains to lock the door first.

Fucking idiot.

Heat flushed through my body as I stomped to my

condo a few blocks away with bunched fists balled at my sides. A blaze of fury engulfed me so fully that I was certain passersby on the street could see steam smoking from my ears.

Back at the condo, it didn't take long before I was gathering Tye's things and throwing them into trash bags. Only stopping to toss the bags into the hallway for a courier service to pick up and deliver to his office.

Approximately forty-five minutes later, I'd successfully removed any semblance that Tye Smithgerald Jerod III had been in my life and it was only then that I allowed my fury to melt into embarrassment.

Ten years I'd been with him and *that* was how our relationship ended? At noon on a random Tuesday in February, a decade long chapter of my life came to a close within the span of an hour.

Unbelievable.

A suffocating sensation tightened in my throat, but I managed to push it down long enough to call the building's maintenance team and ask them to come change the locks right away. And I made damn sure they billed the rush charge to Tye's credit card.

It had been ten months since that fateful day, yet it still felt like a fresh blow to the stomach every time I flashed back to the grueling memory.

And while I hated to admit it, instead of coping with the breakup like a normal person, I'd become a recluse. The kind of person who locked herself in her office and threw herself into the thick of work twenty hours out of the day… every day.

My friendships faded months ago. And if it weren't for my half brother and his family coming to stay at our vacation house in Malibu a few times this past year, the likelihood that I would've had social interaction with anyone outside of the office was slim to none.

I'd clocked more hours in the last ten months than I had in the eleven years since Ben and I started the company. While I wasn't exactly proud of my lack of a social life, I had the accomplishments to make up for it. Like finally landing a coveted spot at Paris Week of Fashion this past winter and showcasing two collections of our most detailed haute couture pieces to date.

We'd made it into Miami Week of Fashion a few years back and even headlined the New York shows for the last three, but becoming a key show in Paris… that's when a designer knew they'd reached the peak of their success.

I should've been riding the high of being named one of the "top up-and-coming fashion designers in the world" by nearly every major media outlet in the world — rightfully so, might I add—but with the holidays approaching, all I could feel was a ripple of emptiness settling into the depths of my bones.

No matter how tirelessly I worked day in and day out, I knew when I shut my laptop at the end of the night and laid my head down against my pillowcase, the hollowness inside would consume me whole.

It always did.

So, like any rational person who wanted to avoid their own personal purgatory, I laid in bed tucked snugly beneath a cloud cotton duvet while mindlessly scrolling Socialgram at two in the morning.

There was something about living vicariously through the highlight reels of the friends and acquaintances I used to hang out with that made me feel like we were still connected in a way.

Oh look, Barrett acquired another business. *Scroll.*

Stella was moving to Chicago. *Scroll*. Samira won another golf tournament. *Scroll*. Tye was engaged. *Sc*—

Tye was *what*?

I thumbed my way through the carousel of images half a dozen times to ensure I wasn't hallucinating—spoiler alert; I wasn't—before re-reading the caption a second time.

Proposed to my beautiful fiancée, Candace, on our one-year anniversary. Wedding next summer. You're all invited! #TyeingTheKnot

TYE WAS ENGAGED.

En—fucking—gaged.

Ten months after we ended our *ten-year* relationship? Based on that fact alone, I guessed it took him—what?—half a business day to grieve our relationship before moving on.

It took the guy eight years to propose to me and another two of avoiding the topic of wedding planning and now he was engaged to this—this whore!

Before I could fully process what was happening, I was out of bed and pacing back and forth on an endless loop in front of the footboard. I racked my brain trying to come up with a scenario to explain the monstrosity that was my life.

Shit, I really needed to stop hanging out with my sister-in-law. Her pacing problem was really starting to rub off on me.

I took a deep breath to gather my composure.

Tye was engaged. With a wedding date set. While I, on

the other hand, couldn't spend five minutes alone with my thoughts before seeking a distraction. And this entire time he'd been out there happily moved on for… how long? I reread the caption again and my jaw dropped open.

How were they celebrating their one-year anniversary? We broke up *ten* months ago!

Obviously, I knew the guy was a cheater, but getting into a new relationship two months before ours ended… that was low, even for him. And to add an extra splash of drama to the pot, his new fiancée wasn't even the secretary I found him fucking in his office.

How many other women had there been before I caught him?

Nope, nope. I quickly retracted the thought as bile rose in my throat.

"Fuck, fuck, fuckity, fucking, fuck!" I screamed to no one and the sound of my rage echoed off the walls of my room.

Shit, I guessed I needed to stop hanging out with my brother, too. The guy used the word "fuck" like it was the only one in the dictionary and apparently I'd adopted his nasty habit.

I let out a pent-up breath and slumped down onto the edge of the bed, hanging my head in my hands.

I hated myself for not figuring out his lies sooner. And even worse, for still caring about him all these months later. But when you already wasted a third of your life on someone, what was another year of heartbreak added to the mix?

"Ughhh," I groaned, flopping back onto the mattress.

I needed a break. A big fat break.

From work. From life. From everything.

Turning over to the nightstand, I let out a sigh as I reached to grab the purple-colored pill bottle I'd come to know well and twisted off the top. Shaking the bottle, I watched as two giant sleeping pills plopped into the palm of my hand.

There was no way I was getting to sleep on my own, and drowning myself in a bottle of tequila at this hour wasn't an option. I could *not* be hungover for our quarterly investor's meeting tomorrow afternoon.

I grabbed the mostly empty glass of water from my nightstand to assist with chasing down the pill before slipping the silk eye mask over my eyes. Nuzzling underneath the duvet comforter, I waited until the sleeping pills worked their magic, eliciting a warm buzz of tranquility beneath my skin.

Using every thought-blocking technique in the book, I slowly, slowly began drifting to sleep. On the brink of slumber, I silently prayed to whatever gods may be that when I woke up in the morning, all of this would be a horrible dream.

BEEP. *BEEP. BEEP.*

Seething, I threw a hand out of the warmth of my covers, desperate to end the source of my agony. What time was it anyway?

I peeled an eyelid out from my sleep mask and winced at the stream of sunlight pouring through the curtains and straight into my eyeballs. Well, the sun was already up, so it had to be at least six.

BEEP. BEEP. BEEP.

"Shut up!" I grumbled at the deafening noise, flailing a

hand over the nightstand until I grasped my phone. I answered the call flashing across my screen and the megaphone-worthy beeps ceased, finally putting an end to my suffering.

"Get your ass up, Aera! Why did *today* of all days have to be the one you picked to be late?" Ben's hushed voice sounded through the speaker. While I might've been half asleep, I didn't miss the bridled anger laced in his tone.

My business partner must've taken up post as the village idiot if he thought calling to yell at me this early in the morning was going to work out in his favor.

Plus, I wasn't even late yet. I still had a full hour to get to the office for our leadership team's morning debrief, and even then, I'd still be two hours early compared to our nine to fivers. If Ben was going to be pissed at me for sleeping in an hour later than normal, so be it.

I pressed the red button in the middle of the screen and hung up on him without an ounce of remorse.

My eyelids fluttered closed, calling me back to my delicious slumber. But right as I got myself tucked perfectly into the warmth of the comforter, the beeping returned.

I could see it now. Today's newspaper headlines would read:

World-renowned fashion designer, Aera Chase, murdered her longtime business partner, Benjamin Fletcher, in a brutal display of vengeance. Click here to read the grueling details about how she chopped off each of his extremities one by one—penis included.

FEELING MY BODY TEMPERATURE RISE, I snatched my phone and slammed it against my ear. "Ben, if Christ himself isn't coming back at this very moment, I swear to fucking god I'm going to murder you," I grumbled into the receiver with a scowl plastered on my face, which he, unfortunately, wasn't able to witness.

"Christ, swearing, and murder in the same sentence? How becoming of you, Aer."

"Get to the point of your call before I hang up on you a second time."

"You're late to our meeting with the investors," he spit venomously. Ben had always been an ass, but he wasn't one to take a vicious tone with me, especially when he was joking around. "I've been stalling for the last half hour, telling people you're having car troubles, but it appears you've taken it upon yourself to sleep in until noon instead. What the fuck, Aera!" he whisper-yelled.

"It's not noon, you imbecile. Our board meeting isn't for another…" I trailed off, twisting my head to get a better view of the clock on my nightstand—12:32 p.m.

I shot up straight in the bed. "Start the meeting. I'll be there in twenty." I hung up the call before he had the chance to respond with another snide remark.

Eighteen minutes later, I strode through the conference room door with a lug wrench in hand and an ashy-colored stain smeared on the front of my shirt.

It was moments like this that made having a condo within walking distance of the office worth the outrageous price I paid for it. I tried not to imagine how much worse this situation would have been if I'd stayed at the Malibu house last night like I'd originally planned to until I got swept up at the office.

"Sorry, boys. I got a nasty flat on the freeway and not a

single one of those pesky East Coast transplants were willing to stop and help a girl out." I shook my head and waved the lug wrench around in a circle.

The investors, most of which unfortunately happened to all be middle-aged white men, stared at me with bug eyes, like they hired me to recreate a scene from their favorite porno.

Their wives must be so proud.

"Color me impressed, Miss Chase," Todd, one of our biggest investors, piped up from the furthest end of the conference table after a beat. "I don't even know how to change a tire myself. How honorable of your parents to teach you how to change one."

Of course Todd didn't know how to change a tire. The guy came out of the womb a billionaire. I'd be shocked if he'd ever set foot behind the wheel of a car before for anything more than a picture. If I was a betting woman, I'd say he had, hmm… five drivers on standby at all times? If not more.

"Oh, enough about silly old me." I gave them all a sweet smile and turned my attention to Ben, who stood at the front of the room in his perfectly tailored navy-blue suit with a scowl on his face as usual. Basking in the magnificence of my power, I shot him a knowing wink, "Ben, where were you?"

"NICE SAVE." The corners of Ben's lips twitched upward the slightest hair once we were alone in the conference room. "The lug wrench really sold it." A deep laugh he let few people hear bellowed out of his chest as he grabbed the wrench off the table and waved it above his head like a rodeo clown.

"What? I had to make it seem believable! *And* it got Todd to put up another half a million on his initial investment, which I consider a success." I lifted a hand to high-five Ben, but he left me hanging.

Typical.

"True." He relaxed down onto the edge of the long, rectangular table. "Hey, if shit hits the fan for us in the future, you could make a killing as a car salesperson." His elbow nudged into my side as I took a seat next to him.

"If Inamra went down in flames tomorrow, the luxury car dealerships in Beverly Hills would be my first stop," I quipped with a small smile splayed across my lips.

Ben and I met freshman year when we got paired together for a group project for one of our general electives. From the start, there was no denying the instant draw we felt toward one another's opposing skill set. By the end of that year, Inamara was born out of pure ambition, and Ben had become a permanent fixture in every aspect of my life.

He also happened to be the one who set up Tye and me on a blind date. And if he weren't so damn good at running the behind-the-scenes of the business, that reminder might've given me more motive to follow through with the murder charge I threatened him with earlier.

"You good, Aer?" His brows drew together as he twisted to meet my gaze.

"Not really, B." I slouched forward and let out an uneven sigh, swallowing back the tears that pricked the back of my throat. "I'm sure you've heard the news by now…" I trailed off, alluding to Tye's engagement announcement.

"Yeah…" His voice grew quiet while he crossed and uncrossed his arms, struggling to remain still.

I'd known Ben and Tye remained friends after our breakup, and I'd be lying if I said it didn't hurt. But I also knew that if Ben ever had to choose between the two of us, he'd pick me. Every single time. Though I'd never make him do it.

Ben swore he hadn't known about Tye's infidelity, and I believed him. I knew he still felt guilty about setting us up in the first place, although he never could've predicted how it'd end.

He might've been a bit of a grump sometimes, but I knew he always had my best interest at heart. One day he'd make some girl out there really happy, but that girl sure as hell wouldn't be me.

I cringed at the thought of having to kiss him. *Disgusting.* Or worse, have sex with him. I shuddered inwardly at the thought. *Revolting.*

"I think I need a break." A huff expelled from my lungs after I took a minute to breathe through the dull ache knotting in my chest. "I'm just… a shell of the person I used to be. Outside of work, the only people I talk to are my brother and sister-in-law. I hardly sleep anymore. And I think creativity is taking a hit because of it."

"A break?" Ben replied quizzically, faint amusement flickering in his eyes.

Aside from flying to Florida to visit my brother and sister-in-law every so often, I hadn't been on a *real* vacation since spring break my senior year of college.

When my brother talked me into buying the Malibu house together for family gatherings, I told myself it would be a peaceful escape from work life. Yet, more often than not, when I visited, I'd spent more time in the office upstairs than relaxing on the beach.

I loved my job. I truly did. But last night's wake-up call made me realize that continuing to throw myself into an endless downward spiral over a man who couldn't care less about me was keeping me from living.

Not to mention, the creative lull I was in could've easily killed Inamra's chances of headlining New York Week of Fashion next year. If I kept it up, we'd be out of the running before the officials even began debating which fashion houses to invite.

I needed to get away from this place—my life—and break free from the gloom-filled cocoon I'd been living in the past few months.

"Yup, I think I need to get out of town and do a factory reset on myself, you know?" I babbled, springing to my feet. "I could go on vacation for the holidays… see some snow. Ohhh, maybe I'll go to a place that has a Christmas festival!" I flailed my arms at my sides, and Ben stared back at me with both brows raised as if I'd abandoned every drop of sanity within myself. "Everyone will be out of office for the next few weeks anyway, so I won't even have to think about work!"

A ripple of uncertainty washed over me for a moment as I observed Ben tossing my words through his brain, astonishment spread over every millimeter of his expression. I only stopped myself when he tilted his head to the side and a wide grin pulled up the corners of his lips.

I knew he'd come around eventually… even if it was only for the benefit of getting me out of his hair for a few days.

Rising to his feet, Ben waltzed over toward the

doorway and paused to look back at me before crossing the threshold to the corridor, which led to his office. "Not a bad idea, Aer." He shrugged. "Who knows, maybe it'll be the best damn thing that's ever happened to you."

His words sent a wave of relief flooding over me.

I sure as hell hoped he was right.

2

AERA

THE MIDNIGHT HOUR crept closer and my sleep deprivation worsened with each passing minute. Moonlight shone brightly through my home office windows, illuminating my workspace, which was cluttered with sketchbook drawings and fabric swatches.

I was only a few tweaks away from finalizing next summer's collection. However, in the hours since sitting down at my desk, I hadn't done much besides ponder the words Ben said earlier.

Who knows, maybe it'll be the best damn thing that's ever happened to you.

It didn't take much for someone to notice I was in a funk, and a fun-filled holiday getaway seemed like the perfect way to catapult me out of it.

After dwelling on the idea of a Christmas vacation for a bit longer, curiosity got the best of me and willed me to open up a new browser to see what the home swapping website I came across on Socialgram was all about.

I'd always suspected these apps were listening in on my conversations based on the *conveniently* timed advertisements that popped up mere hours after I'd mentioned something in passing, yet knew for a fact I'd never looked up before.

Seriously, how else would they have known I was looking for a vacation rental? It was just plain creepy.

I perused through the listings on the site, slightly disappointed at the abysmal selection there was to choose from. Most of the houses were fine, but I didn't want *fine*. If I was going to abandon work for the better half of a month, I wanted the place to be perfect.

A gag nearly escaped my lips when I came across a listing which required the guest to share a bed *with* the homeowner. It also didn't help that the lister's profile photo resembled a flaccid penis.

A cringe crawled up my spine at the sight. What kind of sick fuck would post that? *Reported.*

Well, if this idea failed, I could always show up on my brother's door step unannounced. Although, the last time I did that, he nearly had a heart attack at the ripe age of twenty-eight.

Not to mention, Abel played professional football in Miami and Florida wasn't exactly my idea of a winter vacation spot. And as much as I loved my new-to-the-world nephew, Emerson… I'd rather not spend my time off work listening to him cry and wail between his momentary spats of cuteness.

Not to mention, I already saw the boys and my sister-in-law, Scarlett, last week when they came to spend Abel's bye week at the beach house.

Well, it was safe to say that idea was off the table.

I let out an exasperated breath and went to exit the website but stopped right before hitting the little red "X" in the corner when a brand-new post caught my attention.

New Listing:
Comets Valley Cottage

The perfect holiday getaway for someone looking to break away from the mainstream of life and enjoy the holidays in a town the Christmas Channel movies could only dream of replicating.

OKAY... creepy.

I was, in fact, looking to break away from the mainstream of life, and very much wanted to enjoy a town that looked like it was straight out of a Christmas channel movie.

Were these apps capable of listening in on my thoughts too or something?

Either way, the thought didn't stop me from opening the notification and perusing through the professional photographs. I had to applaud the lister for not posting pictures which appeared to be taken through a smudged smartphone lense like most of the other listings.

The cottage was a cute, assumedly quaint two-bedroom based on the carousel of images. It had a charming living area and kitchen equipped with modern appliances. But it was the final few slides with images of the town plastered in string lights and holiday decorations that really sold me.

This was exactly what I was looking for.

Thank you internet mind readers.

I clicked on the lister's profile, who thankfully did not have a profile photo of an erogenous body part. Instead, the photo was a simple headshot of a darling early twenty-something girl who looked like she spent her weekends perfecting her sourdough recipe and crocheting pom-pom topped beanies for the local children's center.

Relief flooded through me when I noticed a bright green dot appeared next to her profile picture, letting me know she was online to chat. Taking in a deep breath, I worked my fingers over the keyboard as I typed out an introduction message.

Aera: Hi, I wanted to see if your house was still available for the holidays? If so, there are pictures of my beach house in Malibu which you'd be staying in.

My housekeeper, Janice, takes care of all the cleaning and if you're extra nice, she might even cook breakfast for you. It's not as good as my sister-in-law's (she's a chef, by the way), but it's still better than cooking yourself. I'm not much of a cook... I burned a cup of noodles last week because I forgot to add water before putting them in the microwave.

Was that too much information?

Anyway, I'm normal. Very normal. And clean. Very clean. I promise I won't burn your house down. The cup of noodles thing was a one time incident, I swear! I also promise I won't go through your personal items.

I'm just a normal, clean, recovering workaholic who's looking for a place to relax over the holidays and maybe go to a Christmas parade or two. Let me know your thoughts!

AFTER I HIT SEND, I read my word vomited message, *which* was a grave mistake, and slapped a palm to my forehead as I sunk back into my chair.

I was a complete and utter idiot.

What kind of person told someone they were normal? Serial killers. Serial killers were the kind of people who felt the need to convince others they were normal.

And why did I sound so professional? "*Let me know your thoughts*"… this wasn't a business meeting. Don't even get me started on the noodles. Why did I think that was necessary?

Three dots appeared on the screen, letting me know she was typing. I slammed my eyes shut and held my breath until I heard the ping from the new message. I peeled my eyelids open, and much to my surprise, I wasn't met with a flat-out rejection like I'd expected.

Juliet: Hi Aera! I looked through your photos and your house is *gorgeous*. I'd love to trade with you for a few weeks.

I'm also normal, clean, and have burned a cup of noodles or three in college. No crimes that I know of. But I had a sleepwalking problem when I was younger, so I may never know for sure.

You'll be happy to know Comets Valley has an enormous Christmas festival, and it's the highlight of the year. You'll love it! But unfortunately, there aren't many men here though, so if that's what you're in the market for to

help you "relax," you might be better off choosing somewhere else.

Aera: Perfect, who needs men anyway? The less of them, the better. How long should we switch for?

Juliet: Agreed. How does the day after Christmas sound?

I WASN'T sure how safe it was switching homes with someone you had only sent a few messages back and forth to, but I was so desperate for an escape from reality to give it another thought. Even if this Juliet woman lived in Timbuktu…I was willing to accept.

Aera: Sounds great. The sooner we can switch, the better!

Juliet: How about tomorrow?

Aera: Perfect!

JULIET and I exchanged a few more messages with logistics and contact information before I shut down my computer for the night. Crawling into bed, my skin buzzed with excitement as I laid on my pillow and pulled the comforter up to my shoulders.

And for the first night in months, I wasn't kept awake until the early hours of the morning, plagued with never-ending thoughts of what could've been.

I MIGHT AS WELL HAVE CHANGED my name to Alexander, because I was having a terrible, horrible, no good, very bad day. Anyone who claimed vacation was "fun" and "relaxing" was a liar. It was nothing of the sort.

It all started when I dropped by the office to get a few things squared away before leaving on my trip. I stopped at my assistant, Lydia's, desk to tell her I'd be out of town for the next few weeks and that she could take the time off too if she wanted—paid, of course.

And the woman passed out.

Like, fell into a limp heap on the floor right in front of me. I almost had to call the paramedics at seven in the morning, for God's sake.

I'd never seen someone pass out before, and for a moment, I thought I accidentally killed her. I mean, I wasn't entirely sure how that would've been possible, but with an unconscious woman looking lifeless on the floor, I wasn't exactly thinking straight.

Later, as I walked out of the building, one of Inamra's prominent customers, who was on his way to a meeting with Ben, stopped me while I was wearing sweatpants… sweatpants!

I never would've been caught *dead* in sweatpants had I not been in pre-vacation mode.

The guy—I couldn't remember his name… Phil? Jeff? Bob?—gave me a once over and I could've sworn I heard him mumble something to the tune of "whatever makes sales happen" as I walked away.

Loser.

After an unnerving time at the office, all seemed well for a moment as I made my way out of the city and set out on the open road toward Comets Valley.

The drive was eleven hours north of Los Angeles in middle-of-nowhere Oregon, a few miles north of the California border, but I was determined to make it in ten.

Or so I thought until I came to the mistimed realization that I failed to account for two important details in my plan. To start, there was the fact that I had never driven in snow before. And more importantly, that my sports car was in no way designed to be driven on icy roads.

Since this whole vacation was somewhat of a spur-of-the-moment decision, I *might* have forgotten to do some research on the driving conditions before I merged onto the highway. Rookie mistake on my part.

Add in the reality that I rarely ever drove anywhere other than the beach house, and I was screwed. Completely, royally screwed.

What was supposed to take eleven hours rapidly turned into twelve. I primarily spent the last two hours hunched over the steering wheel with a white-knuckled grip. All while, the tail end of the car skidded between both lanes on the back roads which lead to Comets Valley.

My only saving grace was that the other drivers on the road were few and far between.

By the time I made it to the cottage, I was abnormally exhausted from being on edge the last part of the drive that I didn't even stop to take in my surroundings before trudging up the stairs with all my luggage in hand.

I was in desperate need of stress relief, and the only thing keeping me from that was not being able to remember which bag I packed my vibrator in.

After tearing apart two suitcases, my purse, and a duffel bag, I concluded I wouldn't be cumming unless I was going to do it by hand, and that simply *wasn't* an option for me in my current state.

I briefly debated downloading one of those godforsaken dating apps with the hopes of reining in a quickie until I remembered Juliet telling me this town was more desolate than Tristan da Cunha when it came to men.

I fished out a pair of knee-high boots from one of my suitcases—which I should note were the furthest thing from snowshoes—and squished my feet into them with a gripe. Charging down the stairs and out the front door, I began my trek toward the town square from Juliet's pictures.

If I couldn't have an orgasm, the least I could do was grab a snack.

However, it only took the two hundred steps to the mailbox before water had soaked through to my socks. And there were *few* things in life more disgusting than wearing wet socks.

Huffing, I pivoted around on my heels and marched back up the driveway. Once inside, I kicked off my shoes by the front door and dried off the soles of my feet. I pulled my phone out of the pocket of my far-too-thin-for-twenty-degree-weather jacket, then hung it on the coat rack.

Plopping down onto the couch, I opened one of the food delivery apps on my phone and sifted through my options for dinner. After spending a solid twenty minutes internally debating between Momma and Pop's Pizza Kitchen or Comet Queens Cookin' Counter, I decided to order both.

What was the harm in supporting a few local businesses, right?

Twenty minutes later, a knock sounded on the front door, and I hopped up from the couch to open it. Cold air chilled my face and my eyes widened at the sight of two different delivery drivers standing on the front porch with multiple boxes and bags in each of their arms.

"Guys, the food's here!" I called back to absolutely no one.

I was confident both men caught onto my ploy based on the knowing side glance they shared with each other. My betrayal of a stomach growl as I stood in the doorway only solidified what they already knew.

"Thanks so much!" I snatched my food from them and slammed the door shut behind me.

I felt a flush creep across my cheeks once I was alone. Of course, of course this would happen to me today of all days.

Fine. Maybe five pizzas, jumbo bread sticks, a family-size lasagna, and two cobblers—one peach, one blackberry—might have been a bit of an overkill for one person. But I was on vacation, for God's sake! I refused to be shamed by the people of Comets Valley for supporting small businesses!

Popping open one pizza, I took out a slice of pepperoni and shoved half of it into my mouth. Pizza in hand, I poked my head around the living room, trying to find the remote until I spotted Juliet's cat, Mr. Whiskers, erotically rubbing himself against it.

Did I forget to mention there was a cat? And that he had humped *everything* in sight since I arrived. Seriously, everything.

Deciding I wouldn't be touching the remote until I was

able to fully disinfect it, I turned the television on from the button on the bottom and flipped through the channels until I landed on a holiday movie premiere.

With half a pizza down the hatch and a quarter of peach cobbler missing, I started my third Christmas movie of the night. And it was right then when I came to the conclusion that vacation was stupid.

That's right, I said it.

Vacation was stupid.

During the entire first movie, I mindlessly watched while mentally planning the fall collection for next season in my head. And the second movie? Thought about new pitch ideas for investors. Oh, and my plans for the third? You guessed it, jot down ideas for the womenswear shows for Milan Week of Fashion in February.

Even when I was away from work, I couldn't turn off my brain. More than that, I didn't have my laptop or work cell on me to actually get the ideas out of my head and filed away, which was my personal equivalent to hell via brain overload.

How did people do this whole vacation thing? Having this much free time to think and do… nothing was my personal equivalent of having teeth pulled.

I hadn't felt an ounce of relaxation seep into my bones since I woke up this morning, so what was I supposed to do here for a few more weeks?

Nope. Not happening.

I pushed myself off the couch and shut off the television before trotting up the steps—that I'd learned creaked every other stair—and removed my luggage from the guest closet.

Throwing the suitcases on the bed with vigor, I waltzed over and scooped up all the clothes hanging on the clothing rod and threw them inside. Deciding I couldn't be bothered with taking off the hangers, I made a mental note to send Juliet a DollarApp payment to buy some new ones instead.

All was going swimmingly with my escape plan until the zipper on the second suitcase broke off completely.

Why me?

Grabbing a pillow off of the bed, I buried my face into it to drown out the sound of the infuriated scream escaping my mouth. Who would've guessed that the universe *wanted* me to stay in this godforsaken town another moment longer? Not me.

I shoved all of my luggage off of the bed and onto the floor in one swipe, then climbed into bed with a huff before reaching over to switch off the lamp on the nightstand.

To make matters worse, the sheets were scratchy and smelled like someone had drowned them in lavender for weeks on end before tucking them into the bed.

"Ughhh!" I let out a groan and clamped my eyes shut.

I should've known that stupid travel swap ad was too good to be true, because it wasn't every day you fell asleep to the sound of an orange tabby cat masturbating itself with a squeaky toy outside your door.

3

AERA

I SHOT up in bed at the sound of fists pounding hastily against the front door. Still bleary-eyed, I peered over at the clock on the dresser across from the bed, quickly attempting to make out the fuzzy numbers before concluding it was somewhere around two in the morning.

Who the *fuck* could possibly be pounding on Juliet's door at this hour of the night? Had she forgotten to tell her standing booty call that she was leaving town or something? What kind of booty call showed up unannounced, anyway? The name was booty *call* for a reason.

Oh, wait… oh my god. What if this was a robber?

Based on my luck over the last twenty-four hours, that possibility didn't seem far-fetched.

I frantically grabbed my phone from underneath the pillow and dialed my brother's number with shaky fingers. It was five in the morning on the East Coast which was early, but my nephew usually took a bottle around this time, so I took my chances on Abel being awake.

My heart thumped louder with each passing ring that sounded on the opposite end of the line. Fists struck the door once again, and my stomach felt like it was going to drop through the floorboards.

Pick up. Pick up. Pick up.

There wasn't much Abel could do three thousand miles away, but at least if I got murdered I wouldn't be left to be mauled and eaten by Mr. Whiskers until Juliet returned, unless of course, my murderer was a cannibal and wanted me all for himself.

Come on. Come on. Come on.

"Aer? Are you okay?" Abel's voice finally came through the speaker.

"No." I shook my head and closed my eyes. "I-I-I think I'm getting robbed." My voice shook as I whispered into the receiver.

"You're *what*?"

"Abel, I'm getting robbed, and the guy sounds huge, so I'm probably going to die." I began hyperventilating with tears welled in the back of my eyes. "I wanted to call and tell you that you're the best brother ever. You'll have to break the news to my mom—it's dinner time in Seoul, so she should answer—, but tell her I love her. Tell Scar and Emerson I love them too." I sniffled, wiping away a stray tear from my cheek.

"Fuck!" he rasped out. "You're not going to die on me like this, Aera. I refuse to accept that lame-ass death speech because you're Aera fucking Chase, and you're not giving up this easily."

"Yes, I am."

"No, the fuck you're not. Where are you right now?"

"In bed, and the intruder is banging on the front door… loudly." Almost as if on cue, another stream of knocks pounded against the door.

"So he's not in the house yet?"

"No."

"Okay, Aer, listen to me. You're going to keep me on the phone, but you're going to crawl out of bed and quietly walk to the closest exit. Grab a weapon on the way, even if it's just a knife from the kitchen, and keep it with you. Got it?"

"Got it." Slowly peeling the comforter off my legs, I crept out into the dark hallway. Careful not to make too much noise, I tiptoed down the steps, doing my best to work around every other stair to avoid creaks. Once safely downstairs, I grabbed a softball bat that was conveniently located behind the coat rack.

Wait, why did she have one of these by the front door, anyway? Oh shit, robberies *were* common around here, weren't they? Of course they were! What the hell was wrong with this place?

"Abel, I'm so scared. The only way out is the front door."

"You can do this, Aer. You're not a fucking quitter."

"I'm not a quitter," I mumbled his words of encouragement back to myself.

I took a deep breath and set the phone down on the ground when the pounding sounded at the door again, causing me to jump backward.

"Who are you? What are you doing here? Breaking and entering is a crime, you know!" I shouted as I inched closer to the doorway, rearing the bat behind my shoulder, prepared to strike my unknown visitor's head if needed.

A male voice grumbled from the opposite side of the door. "Open the door, Juliet. *Please*." The desperate "please" that escaped from the criminal's lips almost sounded like it was paired with a sob.

If the Comets Valley crime syndicate was praying on

their victims by sounding abysmally helpless in order to get their prey to "help" them before making their attack... then this guy was nailing it.

It was probably wrong to open the door for a criminal, especially since this wasn't my house to begin with, but whoever was on the other side of the door seemed like they needed someone's help.

Probably a shrink's, but I'd have to manage in the interim.

Fists rapped against the door again, only this time the knocks held less power, they almost seemed... powerless. Not to mention, my intruder was now *sobbing* on the other side of the door based on the sound of it.

I let out a measured breath and inched closer to the door, deciding to take my chances this wasn't a criminal due to the fact that they knew this was Juliet's home.

Although, stalkers could *easily* find out that kind of information. Hell, anyone with the internet could probably find out this was her house, couldn't they?

However, if this person was a good stalker, hopefully they'd know by now that not only had she left town, but that someone else was inhabiting her house too.

Wanting a look at my criminal—to make it easier to pick them out of a lineup later, obviously—I ducked to the floor. Lifting my head just enough to peer out of the side-light, I found a weeping man—scratch that, a *gorgeous* weeping man—slumped against the front door as he wiped the tears out from underneath his eyes.

What the...

My intruder had a clean-shaven jawline and thick brown hair that looked freshly cut. He was sitting, but his legs looked long. I made a rough guess that he had to be six foot... maybe an inch or so more?

"Please, Juliet." The stranger sobbed into his hands.

I'd come to two conclusions from my initial inspection: First, this man looked like the furthest thing from a criminal. And second, he was probably minutes away from hypothermia because he wasn't wearing a coat or gloves despite the below freezing temperatures outside.

"Aera… Aera… Aera!" Abel's voice boomed from the speaker on the floor behind me.

I crawled over to grab my phone and pressed it against my ear. "Abel, I have to go. I don't think this is an intruder after all. Sorry for waking you."

"Fuck. Don't ever scare me like that again. This is the second time you've almost given me a heart attack." The relief in his voice and his heavy breathing sent a twinge of embarrassment crawling up the back of my neck for accidentally scaring him so badly.

That's what little sisters were for though, right?

"I know, I know," I acknowledged. "Sorry. Tell Emerson and Scar I said hi."

"Will do. Call me later."

Pressing the red circle at the bottom of the screen to end the call, I tossed the phone to the side and then pushed myself off the floor which needed a thorough mopping, by the way. Expelling a steadying breath from my lungs, I gradually inched over to unlock the door, cracking it open ever so slightly.

The last thing I wanted was the man leaning against it to lose his balance and hit his head against the threshold. I was already weary of law enforcement, and the thought of explaining how I concussed my crying burglar seemed like an added nightmare to the one I was already living in.

The man on the front porch flickered his gaze up at me with tears welled in his winter gray eyes. "You're not Juliet," he muttered, running a hand over his nose with a sniffle.

"You're correct…"

"Where's Juliet?"

"Malibu," I responded honestly. "We switched houses for the holidays. I'm staying here for a few weeks and she's staying at my house. We met on a travel home swapping website."

Only after I blabbered to a complete stranger did I realize I *probably* shouldn't have willingly given that information to anyone. It was starting to make *a lot* more sense how people died so easily in horror films now.

Internally cursing myself, I kept the door cracked with my hand on the lock in case I needed to slam it shut on a moment's notice. "Who are you, her ex or something?"

"God no." The man made a noise like he was going to wretch up his stomach onto the doormat. Which likely wasn't far off from reality based on how drunk he was. "Juliet's my sister. My ex's name is Robin, and she's a bitch. I'd rather die than be caught crying on her doorstep at two in the morning."

The criminal, who claimed to be Juliet's brother, stood to his feet and nudged his way through the door. "Juliet keeps a bottle of scotch in the cabinet above the fridge. Be a doll and grab it for me?"

I could smell the alcohol oozing from this man's pores. The last thing he needed was more booze. "You're drunk. And crying. I don't think more alcohol is going to help your cause right now."

"I am not drunk." His steps faltered as he walked into the living room and threw himself onto the couch. "Okay. Maybe a little."

"Why are you drunk exactly?"

"My life sucks," he whined. "To start, my ex—"

"Robin?" I questioned.

"Yes, she left me four months ago." He let out a pent-up breath. "I found a note on the kitchen counter when I got home from work that said, 'Sorry I can't be with you anymore. I'm taking Milo with me.' The woman took my dog. Who takes a man's dog? I loved that dog!"

"Damn." I winced. "The scotch is above the fridge, yeah??"

He nodded.

Standing on my tiptoes, I opened the cabinet above the fridge, and sure enough, there was an unopened bottle of scotch waiting for the taking. He might've thought I got it down for him, but *I* was the one who was going to need a drink if this man planned to pour out his entire life story to me.

If I found out he was a stalker later, I wouldn't feel as bad knowing that he'd done his homework and covered his bases beforehand. But then again, I guessed all stalkers would do their homework before making any moves.

Shit.

"That same week," he started again while I settled onto the couch next to him with the bottle of scotch in hand. "I sold my company. Which isn't a bad thing except for the fact that I don't know what to do now with all the free time I have. I'm going mad—mad!—sitting around watching television all day."

Relatable.

Well, the not knowing what to do with the newfound free time part at least. This guy couldn't be much older than thirty-five, and the thought of giving up Inamra and retiring a few years from now sounded like a nightmare.

"I'll drink to that." I pressed my lips against the bottle

and took a giant swig. The warm liquid rushed down my throat, and my entire body felt tingly after a few seconds. I threw back another drink for good measure before passing the bottle over to my new friend, whose name I still didn't know.

"So, not only am I dogless, girlfriend-less, *and* unemployed… to top it off, I'm homeless too." He slouched lower into the sofa. "I moved back to Comets Valley to be near my family, but there aren't any houses for sale for twenty miles—twenty miles!—Can you believe that? So, now I'm a thirty-six-year-old single man who's living out of my parents' basement." He huffed out a ragged breath that smelled the equivalent of a brewery. "My life is a fucking shit show."

"Dogless… you forgot dogless on the last one. And jobless too."

"Goddamnit!" he wailed, knocking back a long swig of the amber-colored liquid.

"Don't get me wrong, all of that sounds less than desirable, truly. But it doesn't explain why you're crying like… that." I waved my hand in a circular motion over his face.

"There's no reason. I'm just an emotional drunk." He sniffled. "Every time I get this drunk, I weep for no reason. Just endless inconsolable sobbing. I can't help it."

"Remind me to never bring you to a party," I muttered in a low voice.

Although part of me felt bad for saying it because the guy was obviously going through a rough patch. Yet, another part of me didn't feel bad at all though because the guy scared me absolutely fucking shitless in the dead of night all so he could cry on Juliet's couch.

"What's your name?" He handed the bottle back over to me after taking a few more drinks.

"Aera. Yours?"

"Elliot. Want to be friends?" he asked casually, taking the bottle from my hand and throwing back another drink before passing the bottle over to me once again.

"Sure."

Elliot might've startled the shit out of me, but I had to admit seeing someone else suffering made my night the *tiniest* bit better, even if it was a little sadistic. Extending my measly friendship to him was the least I could do.

Well, unless I accidentally befriended a stalker. I wondered how that would hold up if I had to take him to court. Probably not well… not well at all.

"Cool. So, do you have a boyfriend?"

"No."

"Want to have a one-night stand then?"

"Also, no." I passed the now half-empty bottle back to him.

Now listen, the guy was hot. That was a simple fact. But I wasn't *quite* drunk enough to fuck a stranger who I thought was going to murder me twenty minutes ago.

"Understandable." He sighed, taking a long gulp from the bottle. "Want to watch a movie instead?"

"Sure, but you have to be the one to touch the remote."

"Mr. Whiskers's newest conquest?" Elliot asked with a popped brow, to which I nodded my response.

Me and this weird stranger, who I hoped really was Juliet's brother—I made a mental note to check his ID once he fell asleep—sat on the couch together and watched *A Dog's Purpose* while he cried on my shoulder for two hours straight.

Somewhere around four in the morning, I slipped my shoulder out from under Elliot's limp head and replaced it with a pillow, hoping he was too deep in his drunken sleep to notice the difference. I threw a fuzzy accent blanket over top of him, then tilted his head to the side so he didn't choke in case he regurgitated the contents of his stomach.

Quietly creeping up the stairs, I walked down the hall toward the guest bedroom and crawled underneath the sheets, ready to sleep off the last few hours of emotional overload. On the bright side, I wouldn't be needing any sleeping pills.

If the past twenty hours were any sign as to what the rest of my trip would be like, then the next "relaxing vacation" I had would be when I walked through the pearly gates.

As I rode the brink between wakefulness and deep, divine slumber, the sound of Mr. Whiskers making love to a Staples Easy Button woke me again.

"That was easy. That was easy. That was easy." Sounded from down the hall incessantly.

Groaning, I decided that once the sun rose, I would whip my car out of the driveway so speedily my tires would screech, waking the whole town.

This vacation was *over*, and no amount of convincing would prevent me from leaving.

4

ELLIOT

MY BRAIN POUNDED against my skull as sunlight made its way through the slim opening in the curtains and memories from last night slowly flooded to the forefront of my brain.

Robin calling. Booze, lots of booze. Drunkenly stumbling to Juliet's place instead of my parents' house. The most stunning girl I'd ever seen opening the door. Me asking her to have a one-night stand…

I winced at the last one.

In my normal headspace, I never would've asked a woman such a crude question. That was especially true for the women of Comets Valley, most of whom I'd known since kindergarten.

Comets Valley was a small, incestuous town where everyone knew everyone and nothing—not one thing—out of the ordinary went undiscussed by *all* the townspeople.

It was an odd place, really.

Had I not grown up here, I would've despised the place with my entire being. At eighteen, I swore I'd never come back. Yet anytime I had extra vacation time or a major holiday was approaching, I'd always find myself sitting behind my desk with a browser tab open, perusing flights while I was supposed to be on a conference call.

I'd spent the last eighteen years living in New York, building the fastest growing real estate empire in the city. An empire that I had no intention of leaving until the Banks brothers offered an obscene amount of money to acquire the business.

I might've had hundreds of millions in my bank account, but that didn't negate the fact that I was still the jobless loser who got wasted at my hometown's only bar before passing out on my sister's couch.

Aside from the centurion black card in my wallet, my life wasn't that different from the townies who only left this place for their once-a-year beach vacation.

Grumbling at the reminder, I peeled open an eyelid to find the girl from my haze-filled memories sitting on the hand-me-down accent chair I gave my sister years ago. I knew Juliet's cottage was a quaint thousand square feet, but the minuscule amount of space between this stranger and me suddenly made it feel suffocatingly small. Almost as if the walls were closing in on us.

But then again, that could've been the hangover talking. Or the girl staring at me as she took a sip from her steaming mug was the culmination of all of my desires in human form. My brain was a bit too foggy to figure out which though.

Idly taking my time waking, I raked my eyes over the stunning dark-haired woman sitting across from me. Based on my observations, I had a hunch she was around five foot eight, give or take an inch.

It wasn't long before I was imagining those long legs

CHRISTMAS IN COMETS VALLEY

wrapped around my waist. All while I fisted that long straight black hair that flowed to the small of her waist as she rode me.

She was ethereal and delicate in all the right places, but it was the hint of a spark ignited behind her eyes that gave me the inclination that she was far from either of those things.

Even now, in my sober, fully woken state, she was still the most gorgeous girl I'd ever seen. There were beautiful girls, and then there was her. In a league of her own.

"Did we…" I trailed off, deciding it best to break the prolonged silence that passed between us. There was never an easy way to go about asking someone whether the two of you fucked the night before, so might as well rip the Band-Aid off.

She shook her head and nursed another sip from her mug. "The closest we got was you insisting on taking off your pants halfway through watching *A Dog's Purpose*… your movie choice, by the way. You said your pants were making you feel 'confined from your true self'."

I glanced downward at my bare legs and black boxer briefs, which had grown tight from my pronounced morning wood. I plucked one of the throw pillows that was next to me and threw it over my lower half. Although, in retrospect, it hardly mattered since she'd already seen everything, anyway.

Shit. Why did I have to think about her riding my cock?

My little voyeur's lips curled up into a smile as she watched me squirm.

Drunk Elliot was an alter ego that rarely ever came out to play, but when he did, he came out full force. Often-times, the night either ended up with me crying hysterically on a friend's doorstep or in a holding cell. Neither of which was an ideal way to end a night.

"God. Did I..." My words dropped off, trying not to confess to my drunken crying episodes unless she'd already been witness to one.

"Yeah…. a lot."

I slapped a hand against my forehead and ran it down my face with a rugged breath. Great, this was just great. I tossed a few ideas around in my head, pondering ways I could redeem myself, but nothing came to mind.

She was gorgeous, and I was the idiot who cried myself to sleep half naked on the couch.

"You also gave me the whole dogless, girlfriend-less, jobless, homeless spiel as well," she added smugly, shifting lightly in her seat.

Well, there certainly wasn't going to be any chance of redemption after that.

If I had words, I would've muttered them under my breath, but I was too appalled at my actions to formulate any. A humiliating, deflated feeling came over me as I processed how I got myself into this situation to begin with.

"So… how long are you in town for?" I asked, knowing that changing the subject would be the only way to make it out of this with some sense of pride left.

"A few weeks," she hummed, taking another swig from her mug.

"I take it Juliet used one of those home swapping services again?"

"She didn't tell you? She's staying at my house in Malibu until after Christmas."

"She's staying for the rest of the month?" I arched a brow at the girl whose name I was trying to remember.

Juliet had always been a free spirit, but leaving her life here for a couple of weeks without telling anyone seemed out of the norm, even for her. Part of me wondered if the reason she left was because she found out the results of her graphic design fellowship.

My sister was ten years younger than me, so we weren't super close growing up. But since moving back to Comets Valley in August, she's easily become my best friend. Then again, aside from a few high school buddies, there weren't all that many people to befriend here, anyway.

"Yeah, but I'll be leaving tomorrow."

"Not a fan of small towns?"

"I haven't even walked to town yet, but after the day I had yesterday trying to get here, I've seen enough to know that I won't be staying," she replied matter-of-factly.

"You can't leave without going downtown first. It would be a waste of a trip if you didn't get to experience the best part of this place."

She gave me an unamused shrug. "You probably don't remember this, but yesterday you agreed to be my friend, and I wanted to see if you were still interested."

My brain malfunctioned, and I stared at her dumbfounded and wordless once again.

I couldn't decide if it was because of the hangover or the woman in front of me continuously knocking me off my game. Or that the woman who consoled me while I was weeping and complaining last night *still* wanted to be friends.

My bets were on the latter.

"You still want to even after…" I couldn't let the words escape my lips.

"Yeah, might as well," she replied offhandedly. "I don't

have very many anyway, and seeing as you spilled how shitty your life was—your words, not mine—I have a feeling you could use someone too."

Great, now she was offering me a pity friendship. At this point, I was more worried about what I *hadn't* told her last night. Had I told her about my hemorrhoid surgery two summers ago too?

"If you're wondering if you told me about your hemorrhoid surgery… the answer is yes."

"Fuck," I muttered under my breath. "As much as I would love to be friends with you, unfortunately, for the sake of my sanity, I'm going to have to jump into the Grand Canyon."

She let out a small laugh. "You probably don't remember me telling you I had hemorrhoid surgery too. We kind of bonded over it last night."

We bonded over *hemorrhoid surgery*?

"That's just… fantastic."

"Yeah, except for the part where I lied to make you feel better. The closest thing I've ever had to surgery was Lasik a few years ago."

"I wish you would've kept up the lie." I groaned, sinking deeper into the couch cushions.

"So… now that we're officially friends, I also wanted to ask about cashing in your offer for a one-night stand."

I'd never wished I could disintegrate until this moment. I was hoping I made that memory up in my hungover haze, but much to my demise, it was clearly reality.

"I initially said no because we were both intoxicated after breaking out the Scotch," she started. "But now that we're both sober, it doesn't seem like the worst idea if you're still interested."

She stood up slowly from her chair, giving me a full view of her tall and lanky body covered by a black silk robe which cut off at her mid-thigh. And based on the way she tugged it tightly to her chest, it was easy to assume she had nothing on underneath.

She waltzed towards the coffee pot. "Want some coffee?"

Fucking A. That alone was enough to convince me to have that one-night stand with her.

"You're asking me to fuck you?" I croaked out, disregarding the question about coffee, making sure I heard her correctly..

Not that I couldn't believe someone wanted to have sex with me, but it wasn't every day that women came up to me and flat out asked for it. Especially not after a Drunk Elliot episode.

Sure, I had a few girls on retainer back in New York that met my needs, but since moving back home, my sex life had primarily composed of my fist. And until a few minutes ago, that didn't seem like it'd be changing anytime soon.

"Sure, why not? I've never actually had a one-night stand before, but I'm attempting to turn a new leaf in life… and I think a one-night stand would be beneficial in assisting with that."

She made hooking up sound like a business deal, and I was ashamed to admit how much it turned me on.

That's when it hit me. "Forgive me, uh, what was your name again?"

"Aera." She raised her voice to be heard over the sound of the coffee maker pouring its contents into a mug.

The name sounded familiar, but I couldn't place a finger on where I'd heard it before. Maybe she was in real estate? Then again, there were roughly eighty thousand realtors in New York City alone. So even if she was, the odds that I'd bumped into her before were slim.

"Aera, look, you're beautiful, so please don't let the next words out of my mouth make you think otherwise. But I'm afraid I'd be a shitty lay right now."

"Ehh, it would be hard to be worse than my ex, so I'm willing to take my chances."

Hmm, her ex was bad in bed. Noted.

"At least let me take you out to dinner first." I countered in an attempt to convince her to stay in town long enough to get to know her better. "I would say drinks, but after last night, I don't think I'll ever be drinking again."

"Consider our coffee drinks then." She wore a smug smile as she handed me over a ceramic mug with a Moon Pie Festival logo printed on it.

My sister's mug collection knew no bounds. Wherever we went, she had to buy one. We could drive two towns over and she'd find an excuse to buy a mug plastered with images of their most notable landmark.

I sat up on the couch and took a sip, ignoring the burning sensation in my throat as the black sludge slithered down. Much like her taste in mugs, it appeared my sister had shitty taste in coffee as well.

"Tastes like ass, doesn't it?"

"It's disgusting." I winced.

"See, we're already getting along so well," she quipped, settling back into the chair across from me. "We should sleep together now, right?"

"Are you a sex maniac or something?" My brows drew together as I tilted my head to the side.

"Quite the opposite, actually. I haven't had sex in…"

She paused, counting on her fingers. "That's beside the point, but it's been a while."

I hummed, taking in another bitter gulp of coffee.

"There's a blizzard outside right now, and according to the news, we're snowed in until the roads get plowed tomorrow." She let out an exasperated breath. "Might as well make the best of it."

She didn't seem excited about it, but she had a point. Cabin fever would set in, eventually. Though, I couldn't help but wonder if I gave into this fling to help her "turn a new leaf" if that'd only give her more of a reason to drip out of town at the first chance she got.

"Let me think on it over breakfast. Did Juliet leave any food?"

I didn't miss the small pout she sent my way. "Not much, but there's some lasagna and a blackberry cobbler in the fridge."

"Ahh, so you're the one everyone was talking about last night at Sal's Pub."

Darrell and Janson both came into the bar last night after their delivery shifts, and word spread quickly about an outsider being in town. We didn't get many tourists around here, so newcomers were easy to spot whenever they passed through.

"Oh god," she groaned, hanging her head in her hands. "Everyone knows about that?"

The corners of my lips tugged up into a wide grin. "Welcome to Comets Valley."

5

AERA

IF SOMEONE ASKED me on a scale from one to ten how embarrassing it was to blatantly ask a man to have sex with you and then get temporarily rejected, my answer would be an eight out of ten.

The two points of grace were for the fact that I asked him before he had his first cup of coffee. Because I made few logically sound decisions before a steaming cup of liquid gold sent caffeine shooting through my central nervous system.

Maybe it was a bit forward to ask a man who showed up drunk on my doorstep to have a one-night stand, but honestly, I didn't care. I needed something, *anything,* to make this trip worthwhile.

Plus, the fact remained the same that, intoxicated or not, he was the one who asked first.

Elliot and I spent the rest of the afternoon sitting across from each other, watching TV and shoveling endless slices of pizza into our mouths. Conversations between the two of us were sporadic and futile, but I'd be the first to admit that I quite enjoyed the comfortable silence that passed between us.

Well, as much as one could consider the sound of Mr. Whiskers pleasuring himself in the corner and countless Christmas movies with nearly identical scripts blaring from the television screen, silence that is.

Scooping up the final heaping spoonful of blackberry cobbler from the takeout dish, I devoured it in one giant bite. Elliot didn't bother to spare me a glance as he scarfed down another slice of pepperoni pizza.

It was freeing not having to put pressure on myself to morph into someone he could envision a long-term future with since we wouldn't ever see each other again after they cleared the roads in the morning.

There was also something about the possibility of the two of us having a quick holiday hook-up that made my stomach swirl with excitement. And knowing that there wouldn't be "strings attached" only made it hotter.

Hell, maybe if this worked out well, I'd give dating a try once I got back to Los Angeles after all. Or at the very least, make an attempt to find a friend with benefits to pass the time with.

Here's the thing though, as much as I wanted this fling to become a reality, I wasn't going to risk the potential of him turning me down for a second time today. But… I had no problem doing my part in making the proposition sound more appealing to him.

"You're quiet over there." Elliot perked his head up from the couch where he was lying with a half-eaten box of pizza resting on his torso.

"Yeah, I think I'm going to go upstairs for a while." I yawned, stretching my arms over my head.

One of Elliot's brows rose a fraction like he knew something was amiss, but I wasn't going to let his keen eye derail me from my plan.

"Watch Mr. Whiskers for me while I take a nap?" I asked, getting up from my seat and doing a full body stretch this time before groggily ambling over to the staircase.

"You want me to put the lasagna in the oven? I can call you down when it's ready."

"Don't bother," I called down to him once I reached the top step.

Shutting the bedroom door behind me, a tiny smile of defiance unconsciously curved on my lips. Walking into the room, I fished my non-work tablet out of the depths of my un-broken suitcase and flopped back onto the bed.

I opened up a private browser and typed the name of the most well-known adult website into the search bar, then clicked one of the first videos that appeared on the home page. Meanwhile, turning up the volume to the highest level until high-pitched moans and animalistic grunts echoed off the walls.

Laying the tablet beside me on the bed, I sat back on the pillows with arms crossed and ears focused on the sounds beyond the door. It helped me that this house was tiny, so I had no doubts that Elliot could hear what was happening all the way down in the living room.

A few minutes passed, and almost as if on cue, heavy footsteps thundered up the stairs. My heart raced as I contemplated all the possibilities of what Elliot might say when he confronted me.

The way I saw it, there were two ways that this was going to play out. One, he was *really* going to think that I was the sex maniac he accused me of being earlier. Or two, his own desire would act as fuel to question the activities I was taking part in all by my lonesome.

Firm knocks struck against the door, and my mouth quirked with humor as I paused the video before taking my time getting out of bed. I paused for a minute and took a deep breath to hold down my amusement, and clutched the opening of my robe tighter to my chest. Twisting the knob, I stuck my head through the small opening in the doorway.

"Uh, can I help you?"

"What are you doing?"

Bingo, my second theory was correct. And now I had him exactly where I wanted him.

"Nothing." It was a piss-poor lie, and we both knew it.

"Nothing?" Elliot echoed back to me with narrowed eyes.

"If you want to chit-chat, could we maybe do it… later?" I asked, looking back into the room at my tablet which was out of his view.

"I don't want to chit-chat." He took a step closer to me. So close that I had to tilt my head back to look up and meet his eyes. "Now tell me what you were doing."

"I already told you I wasn't doing anything."

"It didn't sound like you were doing nothing."

"What'd it sound like then?" I asked innocently.

Elliot bounced his gaze between my eyes for an extended moment, but I wasn't going to crack. Too many male-dominated board meetings had prepared me for moments like this. He was going to have to try a lot harder if he wanted to intimidate me. His breaths grew deeper as he enunciated his next words, "What. Were. You. Watching. Aera?"

"A video." Which *technically* wasn't a lie.

"What kind of video?" He pushed the door open with his shoulder and barged into the room, heading straight for the bed. Snatching the device off the comforter, his mouth dropped open as he twisted the screen to face me.

"You were watching *porn*?" he asked dumbfounded, like he hadn't known *exactly* what I was doing before barreling in here.

I did my best to keep my face impassive as I lifted both my shoulders. "I will neither confirm nor deny."

"You can't deny it when I'm holding the evidence right here."

"It's a virus," I lied.

"A virus that you've been watching for…" He tapped his pointer finger on the tablet, revealing the video progress bar on the bottom of the screen. "… eight minutes and fifty-four seconds?"

I shrugged once again.

"You were getting off to this, weren't you?" He drug his gaze up to the title of the video. '*Getting shared by my boyfriend and his best friend.*' That's what you like to watch… threesomes?"

Actually, no. Not at all.

Dammit, I knew I should've taken the time to find something better, but I was too eager to see his reaction to care. Suddenly flustered, I didn't say a word in response. Instead, I kept my stare firm on his while trying to hide the onset of nerves that were swirling in my stomach.

"Aera, answer me."

"Yes." I should've felt bad for lying so much, but knowing I'd never see him again after this made it *slightly* easier to stomach.

"And you didn't ask me to join you because…"

"Well, you turned me down this morning, so I assumed

you weren't interested." I crossed my arms tightly against my chest.

"I didn't turn you down. I said I wanted to think on it."

"And have you? Thought about it?"

"I'm interested." Elliot crossed the room in two giant steps, closing the gap between the two of us. "Very interested."

We stared into each other's eyes without saying a word, and the tension that soared between us felt as if it were tangible. My body ached for his touch, and the tight knot within my core begged for more.

"Prove it," I challenged after a beat.

Elliot locked his gaze on mine for another long moment, and I held my breath, counting the seconds that passed. Finally, he lifted his hands to cup the sides of my face and crashed his lips against mine.

Our kisses were hasty and reckless from the start, and I lost myself in the way his demanding lips captured mine. I instinctively wrapped my hands around his back and slipped them underneath the hem of his shirt.

I heatedly glided my fingertips across his firm back muscles until the need to feel more of his bare skin on mine took over. Lifting the bottom of his shirt upward, he pulled away from my lips just long enough to grab the back collar of his shirt and tug it over his head.

He flung it onto the ground, and I instinctively trailed my hands sensuously over his hardened abs while I reclaimed my lips, and the passion in our kiss multiplied.

Desire pulsed through my veins as Elliot walked us backward through the room until the back of my knees hit the edge of the bed. He kept our lips cemented together as he lowered us down onto the mattress.

We hadn't done anything more than kiss, and this was

already twenty times better than any experience I had with Tye. Yet, there was a small prick of doubt in the back of my head that was trying to convince me that this time wouldn't be any different from my prior experiences.

Elliot settled his hips between my thighs, and I opened my mouth, allowing more room for his tongue to explore. One of his hands began slowly trailing down my neck and over my breasts until he reached the strings that were keeping my robe together.

"Yes?" Elliot rasped, breaking our lips apart for the briefest of moments.

I hummed my approval, and he untied the knot with one hand. Moving the material to the sides, my bareness was exposed to him, and I watched as he raked his heated gaze over my willowy figure.

He dipped down to my mouth again, and I could feel the smug grin on his lips as he brushed his lips over my skin until he was placing sloppy kisses against the hollow of my neck. "I've been trying to figure out if you were naked under here all day."

"Now you know." I let out a small laugh, gripping the hair at the base of his neck.

"My only regret is not finding out sooner." Elliot shot me a wink before dropping lower to suck one of my hard, rosy nipples between his lips. I let the wave of desire I was feeling settle into my core as I watched him knead my other breast with his palm.

My head lolled back against the pillows as he repeated the same motions on the other side. Soon after, he reached one hand down to my inner thighs and began massaging the soft, sensitive skin. Arousal rushed out of me as he inched his fingers closer and closer to my slit.

"Open up for me," Elliot rasped, and I willingly

obliged. He dipped his middle two fingers in my arousal and spread the wetness up to my clit. "You're already soaked for me."

"You must've forgotten that I was soaked before you got here."

A tumultuous chuckle rumbled out of his chest and he moved upward so his hot breath swept over my ear and sent a prickle of goose bumps down my arms. "You and I both know there wasn't a drop of wetness spilling from your pussy until I walked into this room."

My mouth curled into a knowing smile which he quickly wiped off with a deep, lingering kiss. Our tongues thrashed together as our breaths grew shallow and desperate.

Elliot slid two fingers inside my opening, and a shock wave traveled throughout my entire body. A breathy moan escaped my lips as he worked in and out of me. Again. And again.

"You're going to look so good when you come on my fingers," he whispered against my lips.

My eyes flew open, and I instantly tensed at his words.

"Wait, stop!" I said frantically, and Elliot immediately backed off me. "I've never had a… you know, with anyone," A murmur slipped from my lips as I bit the inside of my cheek. I knew with absolute certainty my pale complexion had turned ghost white.

"No one's ever given you an orgasm?" Elliot lifted a brow in question.

I shook my head side to side, not wanting to elaborate further. I was already ruining the moment with the confession, and giving him the intimate details wasn't going to reignite things back to where they'd been a few seconds ago.

"But you've given yourself one before, yeah?"

I nodded up and down this time.

I knew this wasn't something to be shy about. If anything, it said more about my ex than it did about me, but I didn't want Elliot to think I wasn't enjoying myself if he was able to detect my subpar attempt at a fake orgasm.

"We're not leaving this room until you have at least two, and don't even think about faking it because I'll know."

"How?" I knotted my brows together.

"I'll know." He replied with a sense of calm and ease. Though he didn't hide the arrogant smirk that basked on his face. "Now lie on your back and relax your muscles."

Relax? If I knew how to relax, I wouldn't have been in Comets Valley in the first place.

"Don't worry, I'll help you through it. Start with your face and release the tension in your muscles," he coached, sensing my hesitation. "Good girl. Now unclench your jaw and drop your shoulders. That's it. Now work your way down to your toes until your whole body feels loose."

"I might fall asleep if I stay like this too long."

"Trust me, you won't. You'll be *fully* awake here in a few minutes." My eyes were still closed, but I could practically hear the wicked smirk that played on his lips. "I'm going to kiss you again, okay?"

"Mm-hmm, please."

Elliot gently brushed his lips over mine before placing a tender kiss against my lips that melted my resolve. Then he kissed my chin and the space between my breasts before taking his time planting hypnotizing kisses down my stomach until he reached my center.

With both his hands palming my breasts, he worked his skillful tongue in long, tantalizing licks up and down my slick wet heat. Sucking in a breath, I lifted my hips, desperately craving his tongue on my most sensitive spot.

Sensing my desire, Elliot locked his lips around my clit and a whimper slipped from my lips as he worked his tongue in unhurried circles.

"I like that," I mumbled with a breathy moan.

He kept up the same motion which only made my moans grow louder until I was unabashedly thrusting my hips against his tongue. I could feel an orgasm building underneath the surface, so I focused my thoughts on the new sensations I'd never felt from doing this on my own.

On the rare occasion I was caught between the sheets with Tye, the only thing that would get me to a fraction of this feeling was imagining he was Henry Cavill. But that bubble would burst the second I remembered Henry prob- ably— hopefully—didn't suck in bed.

Shit, shit. I was drifting.

Elliot must've picked up on it too, because he roped me back into the moment by thrusting two fingers inside me while he swirled his tongue around my swollen bud.

"Don't stop!" I moaned so loudly I was certain all of Comets Valley could hear me, but I was too close to coming to give a shit.

Following my order, Elliot didn't stop or change his rhythm even as my inner walls began to contract around his fingers. Keeping his movements steady, he continued to work in and out of me as the most intense orgasm in all twenty-nine years of my life ripped through my body.

Only once my pussy finished convulsing did he slow his pace so I could ride out the final pulses of my high before falling back to reality.

Taking a minute to catch my breath, I lifted my head to meet his eyes. "*That's* what it feels like to not do all the work myself?" I asked with widened eyes and a slacked jaw.

The corners of his lips twitched. "Yup."

"Okay, I'm ready to go again." I threw my head back against the pillow again, and Elliot let out a roaring chuckle.

I was surprised to find myself smiling down at him with softened eyes. Maybe, just maybe, I liked hearing him laugh.

6

AERA

I DOZED in and out of wakefulness, making no convincing attempts to take the full plunge into the day ahead as I soaked up the warmth pressed against my back and extended over my stomach. Curling deeper into the heat, the sheets rustled around me as the heat pulled me in closer.

Oh, my god.

That warmness I felt wasn't coming from the covers… it was Elliot.

My eyes shot open, and I was instantly ripped from the bliss of my dream state and faced with the crushing reality of last night's hook-up staying over.

I remember passing out somewhere after orgasm number three — or was it four?—and *vaguely* remember convincing him that sleeping in my bed would be a lot more comfortable than the couch.

I peered over my shoulder and sucked in a small gasp seeing Elliot's arms contently wrapped around my waist and his shirtless torso pressed against my very naked body.

I slept with a stranger. Oh god, and I *slept* with a stranger.

Even more shocking than that, it was the best damn sex of my entire life. Granted, that wasn't hard to beat, but it was a milestone, nonetheless.

Glancing at the clock, I realized it was only a few minutes past five, which I should've guessed since that was my usual wake-up time for work. Turns out old habits did, in fact, die hard, even on vacation.

Slowly slipping out of bed, I tiptoed to the bathroom to pee and threw on my decade-old *Hitchhiker's Guide to the Galaxy* t-shirt from the dirty clothes pile I made on the floor. It was gross, but my options were limited unless I wanted to wake the man sleeping soundly in my bed.

Thankfully, when I snuck back into the bedroom, Elliot had turned on his side, facing away from me. Carefully peeling back the covers, I crawled back into bed, but not before shoving a king pillow between the two of us as a barrier.

When I woke again an hour and a half later, I felt a sense of relief wash over me when I gazed over to find that the other half of the bed was not only empty, but looked like it hadn't been slept in. If it wasn't for the aching feeling between my thighs, I would've thought that I'd imagined the last fourteen hours.

I rolled onto my back and stared up at the ceiling. A few minutes passed spent trying to gather my thoughts, but the one that stuck out most was how much I missed Elliot's warmth cloaked around me when I woke again. My second thought was consumed by the small pang of sadness, knowing I'd probably never hear his stupid laugh again.

Taking a deep breath, I pushed away the thoughts. I

was leaving today anyway, and the best part about him leaving first was that it saved us the awkwardness of a goodbye.

Peeling back the covers, the crisp December air sent goose bumps prickling across my bare legs. I sauntered over to the closet and pulled out a pair of black sweatpants and a thick gray cardigan from my suitcase and threw them on.

After brushing my hair and teeth in the en suite, I stepped out into the short hallway and bent down to pet Mr. Whiskers before wandering down the steps.

Much to my surprise, when I reached the bottom, there was a tall, half-naked man standing in the kitchen with his back facing me. My mouth dropped open at the sight of Elliot firing up the coffeemaker.

"You're still here," I said in a soft voice, any louder and it would've given away the shock that was laced in my tone.

Elliot turned around, and I could see a flash of surprise flash over his face before he broke into a closed-mouth smile and focused his attention back to the coffee machine. It was a bit reassuring knowing he was equally as startled to see me as I was him.

"I'm making coffee. You want some?"

I nodded, forgetting his back was turned to me. "I, uh, thought you left."

"I was waiting for my shirt to finish in the dryer." He nudged his head toward the small laundry room off the kitchen. "News said they plowed the roads earlier this morning, and I already shoveled the snow off of your car."

"Oh, thanks. You didn't have to do that," I whispered shyly. Before this, I could count on one hand the number of times I'd been shy in this lifetime, but now I was adding a sixth finger over some morning-after chatter? I should've been ashamed of myself.

"I don't mind." He handed me over a coffee mug with an image of dancing Jesus hand painted on it. "You still planning on leaving today?"

Nodding again, I brought the mug to my lips and blew off a bit of steam before taking a long sip which I instantly regretted. "God, this is awful." A disgusted shudder passed through me.

"Yeah… I might've burned it."

No job. No girlfriend. No house. *And* he couldn't make a cup of coffee. Poor guy, at least he knew his way around the bedroom.

"And you're heading back to…"

"Los Angeles," I finished for him, setting my mug down on the table. There was no way in hell I was going to take another sip of that sewer water tasting coffee.

"Right."

"Yeah, I should probably get going if I want to make it back before dark."

"Well, on the off chance you decide to stay, a group of my buddies and I are going to Sal's Pub tonight. Call me if you want to meet up and have a drink or something." Elliot grabbed a pen from one of the drawers and scratched his phone number down onto one of the takeout napkins that was stacked on the kitchen table.

"Or something?"

"Or something," he replied with a smug grin so seductive it made my insides turn to lava. "Drive safe?"

"I-I will."

Halfway out the front door, Elliot called back to me, "Aera?"

"Yeah?"

"I had fun last night." He shot me a wink, and the door slammed shut behind him before I had the chance to reply.

Well, Elliot was gone for good… and he totally left his shirt in the dryer. He might want to add forgetful to his list of shortcomings too after walking home shirtless post-blizzard.

Finally alone, I expelled a deep breath and sunk down onto one of the wooden chairs at the table. That went better than expected, right? Definitely cringeworthy, but it wasn't as painful as I initially thought it'd be.

I might've been cutting my trip short, but I had accomplished spending an entire night without thinking of work for once which was something to be proud of.

Hey, baby steps were still progress.

I DIDN'T WANT to stay in Comets Valley. I really didn't.

In fact, I made it four towns over before realizing I left my stupid tablet on the nightstand and had to turn around to get it.

There were a few minutes where I debated asking Juliet to ship it back to me when she got back to town. But then I remembered what she'd find on my browser if she accidentally opened it up.

And that was how I found myself turning the steering wheel and pressing firmly on the brakes as I pulled into the short driveway in front of Juliet's house once again. Pulling my phone out from my coat pocket, I thumbed out a quick text to her.

Aera: Don't be alarmed if you get reports of a burglar. It's just me dropping back by to pick up something I left.

Knowing how quickly these townies spread news, I had to make sure my bases were covered before I went in so I wouldn't get arrested. A few seconds later, my ringtone beeped, and Juliet's name appeared on the screen.

Before I had the chance to say hello, a feminine, syrupy voice sounded through the speaker, "Aera! I can't believe you're leaving. Oh, and I hope you don't mind, but Ben dropped by to pick up your laptop, and I let him take it."

"Don't worry about it. Hopefully, he wasn't too much of a pompous jerk toward you?" I questioned, silently hoping he didn't insult my new friend.

There was an extended pause on the other end of the line and her voice raised an octave when she finally spoke. "Yeah… he's great. Really great, actually."

Great? Really great?

At this point in life, I arguably knew Ben better than I knew myself and as much as I cherished our friendship, "great" wasn't in the first ten thousand words I'd use to describe his personality.

I gasped. "Oh, my god. You totally had sex with Ben, didn't you?"

"Pshh, no…" she scoffed. "Now, tell me all about how you met my brother. He wouldn't give me the full story, and I want *all* the details."

"Oh no no no, you're not changing the subject!"

"Fine. Ben and I have been hanging out a bit, but there's nothing scandalous to report… yet."

"You with Ben and me with Elliott… I can't believe this," I mumbled to myself.

"Speaking of Elliot…" I could sense the smile in her

tone from seven hundred fifty miles away. "He came by to grab the key from the lockbox after you left so he wouldn't have to mess with it in the dark when he comes back to feed Mr. Whiskers later tonight."

"Shit."

"You'll have to grab the key from him. I think he mentioned he was going to Sal's tonight?"

"Would you mind if I stayed another night?"

"Not at all." I could hear Ben in the background calling her name. "Have fun, bye!"

So as much as I didn't want to stay in Comets Valley another night, I didn't have much of a choice. I wasted so long wrestling with my broken suitcase and forgotten tablet earlier that the sun was setting already. Even if I left again now, it would be early tomorrow morning by the time I made it back to my condo.

The only upside for getting stuck in this hellhole was the hope that I'd be receiving a second round of mind-numbing orgasms from Elliot later this evening.

And even if the night didn't pan out as I hoped, at least my new plans gave me an excuse to go shopping for a new outfit to pass the time.

Grabbing my purse from the passenger seat and locking the car door, I made my way toward the town center Juliet mentioned was roughly a mile walk from the house.

Since when did a mile become so far?

I could've sworn it was a lot shorter than this back in high school when the physical education teachers would force us to run incessant circles around the track.

At long last, I rounded a corner, and the charming town center came into view. My eyes lit up as I watched the townspeople bustle around with coffee cups and shop-ping bags in hand.

Two elderly couples stopped in the middle of the street to hug and chat with each other, and there weren't any drivers honking or screaming expletives out the window demanding they move.

What I loved most though, was the picturesque Christmas tree in the center of the square. And that all the small shops were decorated to the nines like they were in competition with each other.

I stood on the street in awe at the fact that Comets Valley looked identical to the pictures on Juliet's profile. No, scratch that, it was better than the pictures.

For the first time since I'd arrived, a wave of excite-ment flooded over me. Elliot was right. I shouldn't have tried to leave without coming downtown first.

I passed shop after shop with antiques and trinkets before settling on a small boutique on the corner of Main Street. The door to the shop creaked open and a short-haired brunette who appeared to be in her mid-twenties popped up from behind the counter. Her eyes brightened as I knocked the excess snow off of my boots and onto the welcome mat.

"Are you Aera Chase?" she gasped, abandoning the cash register right as another shopper came to checkout.

"That's me." I smiled at her, sticking out my hand and slipping it into her extended one. I instantly drew my eyes to a mannequin in the corner dressed in a deep-cut black blouse that was calling my name. "Could I try that one on?" I nudged my head over to the display.

"Of course you can! My name's Calliope, by the way." She turned back to me with a smile before strolling over to one of the clothing racks. "What brought you to Comets?"

"I was trying to take a quick break from work for the holidays, but it's proving to be more difficult than I thought."

"If I had your job, I'd never take a break. Ever." She beamed up at me.

"I said the same thing, yet here I am." I laughed as she handed me over the blouse and pointed me in the direction of the dressing room. Shutting the curtain behind me, I peeled off the jacket and sweater I was wearing and hung them on the hooks.

"Are you going to Sal's tonight?"

"How'd you know?" I questioned, slipping my arms through the sleeves of the shirt.

"There's not much to do around here on a Saturday night except go to Sal's," she explained. "*And* based on your selection, you seem like you're looking for a date outfit, yeah?"

"I'm sure you know Elliot?"

She let out a small laugh. "Only since kindergarten."

"Really?" I tilted my head to one side while adjusting the top in the mirror. "What was he like when he was younger?"

"He's always been smart, obviously. He was a bit of trouble in high school, partying and whatnot. But in a small town like this, there isn't much for teenagers to do but drink and have sex, anyway."

A laugh spilled from my lips. "Sounds about right." I raked my eyes over my new top in the mirror before pushing the curtain to one side and stepping out. "What do you think?"

Calliope placed a hand on her hip and gave me a once-over while biting her bottom lip. "Something's missing," she said after a beat.

I turned around to look in the mirror again and nodded to her.

She perked up for a second, then waltzed out of sight. "Stay right there. I'll be right back."

A few seconds passed, and she appeared out of nowhere holding up a cherry apple-colored top with a squared neck and exaggerated balloon sleeves.

I sucked in a breath. It was perfect.

She handed me over the hanger, and I instinctively looked inside to see the designer listed on the tag but frowned when I didn't find one. "Do you know who made this? It's stunning."

"Me." She crossed her legs at the ankles and dropped her gaze to the floor for a moment. "I made everything in here."

"Everything?" My jaw dropped as I looked around the store at all the clothing racks filled to the brim with hand-made items. "Well, if you ever decide you want to come work for Inamra, there will be a job waiting for you."

"Really?" she squealed, throwing her arms around me and trapping me in a tight hug. "Thank you, thank you, thank you!"

Twenty minutes later, I was dressed in my newest outfit, and Calliope was leading us down the snow-covered street toward Sal's. A bell chimed above us as she opened the large wooden doors to the town's one and only bar and the two of us shuffled inside.

Stripping off our jackets, we placed them on the coat rack before ambling deeper into the crowded room. There were a few couples sitting at the bar throwing back shots like they were at a frat party, and small groups gathered around bar top tables, munching on appetizers while nursing pints of beer.

"Merry Christmas, Happy Holidays" by NSYNC boomed through the speakers, and the jaw-droppingly handsome barkeep waved at Calliope from across the room.

"That's my brother, Penn," she told me, adjusting the sleeves of her cropped knit sweater. "Let's grab a table, he'll bring us over some drinks in a minute."

I flashed my gaze around the room, hoping that Elliot's winter gray eyes would meet mine. Disappointment felt like a punch to the gut when I came up short.

"He should be here soon," Calliope soothed, grabbing my hand and pulling me toward one of the table tops.

As promised, Penn brought over a tray full of booze and a few appetizers for us to enjoy. And forty-five minutes and a couple of drinks later, I was thoroughly buzzed, yet Elliot was still nowhere to be found.

7
———

ELLIOT

THE BELL above the door outside Sal's Pub sounded as a group of thirty-something-year-old couples stumbled out of the bar and down the now desolate Main Street.

Aside from the one and only gas station on the outskirts of town, Sal's was the only place for miles that stayed open past seven on the weekends. Unless there was a game on, most Saturday nights you could find people gathered in cliques around the bar drinking their asses off as the latest hits thundered through the speakers.

Grasping the door moments before it slammed shut, I swung it open once again. "All I Want For Christmas Is You" by Mariah Carey could barely be heard over the crowd of bar goers singing along terribly off tune.

I paused in the doorway, and a smile tugged up the corners of my lips. It was moments like this that drew me back here after I'd moved away.

After I left Juliet's this morning, I took a quick trip to Seattle to meet with one of my old clients for lunch, and I'd been in such a rush to meet up with Tony and Gabe that I lost my coat somewhere between here and the jet.

First my shirt, and now this. What was going on with me?

Warmth settled into me as I stepped deeper into the room, scanning my eyes across the crowd for my friends. But much to my surprise, in my direct line of sight, there was a lanky, black-haired woman double fisting two shots who had stolen all of my attention.

A smile crawled over my expression as I watched Aera throw back both shots and slam the glasses down onto the table before triumphantly pumping her fists into the air.

Standing there wordless, my heart pounded against the walls of my chest as our eyes locked from across the room. But before I could form another thought, she was beelining through groups of people heading straight toward me.

I hardly had time to brace myself before she threw her arms around my neck and squeezed me like we hadn't seen each other in years. "You're here." Shock coated my voice as I pulled her tighter against my chest.

At some point on my flight back from Seattle, I'd come to terms with the reality that I'd never be seeing Aera again. She hadn't called or texted, so it didn't seem far off to assume she was already halfway back to Los Angeles by then.

Yet here she was, wrapped around me like she'd never left.

"My flight got canceled."

"You drove here."

"I know." She grinned, ungluing herself from me.

Taking my hand in hers, Aera dragged me across the room to her hangout spot. Thankfully, her drinking partner, Calliope, was too engulfed in a conversation with the guys at the next table to notice I was crashing their fun.

"You're also drunk."

"I know that too," she crooned, tossing back a giant gulp of beer from one of the glasses on the table. "We should dance!"

"I do not dance…" I trailed off, standing firm in my place while she swayed her hips to the music.

"Oh, come on, you're telling me you've never gone dancing at a club before?"

"Once," I replied truthfully. "I usually stayed so late at the office that by the time I left, the only thing I wanted was a deluxe cheeseburger and my bed."

"I thought you were unemployed." She knotted her brows together.

"Only as of a few months ago." I smirked. "And the only reason I'm unemployed is because I sold my real estate business, remember?"

Aera gasped like I was sharing information I hadn't already revealed when our roles were reversed. "You're *that* Elliot Peters, aren't you?"

I couldn't help the grin that came over me. "Yes, I'm *that* Elliot Peters."

That made a lot more sense why she didn't want to stick around. If it was me in her shoes, I wouldn't want to continue banging an unemployed dude who lived in his parents' basement either.

"You're rich." Her eyes grew wide like she was telling me a secret I hadn't already known. "Like a billionaire."

"Not quite, but close."

"Holy shit, holy shit! Barrett's the one who acquired your business, isn't he?" she exclaimed, lifting her drink in the air excitedly which caused the beer to slosh around in the glass.

I grabbed the drink from her hand before she spilled it all over herself. "You know Banks?"

That would explain why her name sounded familiar when we first met. He must've mentioned her in passing at some point.

"Of course I do! We went to college together at Warren." She paused for a moment and belched so loudly that a minimum of three people's heads turned to look at her. "Warren Wolves! Woof! Woof! Woof!" she chanted.

I couldn't hold back my laugh as I internally debated who was a worse drunk, me or her. Aside from my occasional weeping episodes, my bets were on her.

"Small world, huh?" I smiled down at her.

"Extremely. Now, dance with me, billionaire boy!" She threw back the rest of her beer before dragging me across the room like a rag doll once again.

There was a small dance floor off to one end of the bar that was primarily used by older couples whenever the band—which consisted of two high school math teachers, an herbalist, and the sheriff—played on Friday nights.

Leaving me in the dust, Aera bolted over to the stage when the chorus of "Santa Tell Me" by Ariana Grande blasted out through the speakers.

Her dancing started off innocent enough as she claimed her spot center stage. But as the song progressed, her moves grew increasingly more sexual until she started sensually pushing down the sleeves of her top.

"Oh, fuck no," I muttered to myself, barging onto the stage the second she reached for the hem of her shirt and lifted upward, exposing her midriff. Mere moments before she flashed half the town, I planted myself in front of her, covering her half-naked body from the crowd. "Aera, put your clothes back on."

"I'd rather wear yours instead." She flickered a seductive gaze up at me while a defiant smile played on her lips.

I narrowed my eyes at her before pausing to pick up the shirt she flung onto the ground. "What're you doing?"

"You know *exactly* what I'm doing. Just like you knew *exactly* what I was doing when you came to my room last night too."

"Afraid to say it out loud?" I challenged, stepping an inch closer to her.

"Fine. I'm flirting with you, idiot."

It only took a few seconds for me to take the black sweater off my back and shove her head through the opening at the top. She stared up at me with a drunken smile plastered on her face while I worked her arms through the sleeves like a toddler.

She was cute when she was drunk.

"Looks better on you, anyway." I shot her a wink and a faint blush rose to her cheeks.

Silence passed between us for an extended moment and all I could think about was how badly I wanted to kiss her again. Even now, in the middle of the bar with half the town watching us. I debated it for a moment longer, but before I had the chance to dip down and capture her lips, Aera hopped off the stage and was lost in the swarm of people.

I stood there dumbfounded for a beat, shaking my head before walking off, bare chested, toward the table we were at earlier. Coming up behind her, I plucked a full shot glass out of her hand. "Nope, I think it's time we get you home."

"Oh, come on," she protested with a scoff. "The night's just getting started!"

I placed my free hand on her hip and ducked down low enough that my lips brushed the shell of her ear.

"You're telling me you don't want to go back to the house and spend the rest of the night coming on my tongue?"

She sucked in a breath, looking up at me while I tossed back the shot of tequila I stole from her with a wink. Placing the glass on the tabletop, I turned to Calliope, who'd been watching us with a wide smile. "Unfortunately, we've got to go home to feed Mr. Whiskers."

"Mr. Whiskers… right." Calliope waggled her brows at the two of us before pushing off her chair to give Aera a quick hug goodbye.

SHORTLY AFTER WALKING out of the bar, I sent my buddies a text letting them know I'd meet up with them another night. Their only response was a picture of a few college girls who were home for the holidays surrounding their table. Rolling my eyes, I shoved my phone into my pocket and ignored them.

On our walk home, Aera insisted on climbing onto my front like a backpack to 'keep me warm'. Somehow turning the fifteen-minute walk to Juliet's place to thirty due to the reality that we kept having to stop and readjust every hundred feet. It might've made things ten times harder, but I had to admit it was pretty damn cute.

Approximately five minutes after we made it through the door, Aera passed out on the couch. Though she made it a point to strip out of the sweater I gave her before settling in for her slumber.

On the bright side, at least I didn't have to sit around

shirtless for the next few hours now that I got my sweater back.

A few hours passed with her out cold, but I continued to watch her out of fear that she was going to wake up and vomit all over the floor. Then there was also the fact that she was so still while she slept, I had to continuously check to ensure she was still breathing.

As she slept, I realized the universe had given me another chance to convince her to stay. Only this time, I wasn't going to leave as easily as I did this morning. She'd already come back once, and the odds she'd do that again weren't in my favor.

That being said, I was willing to pull out any and all stops to keep her here a bit longer.

The sound of Mr. Whiskers tumbling down the steps caused Aera to squirm underneath the fuzzy throw blanket I placed on top of her.

She let out a long yawn before turning her head to look at me. "What time is it?"

"Last I checked, it was a few minutes past midnight."

"And what time did we leave the bar again?"

"Seven forty-five." I pressed my lips together to keep in a laugh.

"And where are my clothes?" She lifted her head to peek under the blanket at her half-naked body. Granted, she was wearing a strapless bra, so she wasn't completely exposed, but the small garment left little for the imagination. "Wait, no. Please don't tell me I…"

"Oh, you did." I leaned back in my chair with a smug smile.

"How many people saw?"

"Half the town, maybe more."

Aera dropped back against the pillows and expelled an

exasperated breath. "I didn't call my ex, did I?" She pinched the bridge of her nose. "I have a tendency to leave him strongly worded voice mails on nights when I've had one too many glasses of wine."

I shook my head. "I take it things ended badly between the two of you?"

"He cheated."

"Yikes."

"With his secretary."

"Oh, damn." I winced, unsure if I should pry for more details or drop the subject altogether. But being the curious-minded person I was, the former won. "And you two were together for…"

"Ten years."

I sat there staring at her with my mouth gaped open.

Ten years?

She mentioned he wasn't good in bed, but how was she with a man for a decade who never once made her finish? More importantly, how the fuck did a man go a decade without realizing his girl wasn't coming? Did he even know where her clit was?

What the fuck.

"I know exactly what you're thinking right now, and I don't know how it's possible either," Aera groaned, twisting onto her side.

"Do you need food or water?"

"No, I feel fine. I only had four drinks and the rest of Calliope's beer, so you saw the worst of it. I might go up to bed and call it a night though." She yawned, getting up from the couch with the blanket still wrapped around her.

"You coming?" She looked back at me, and the smile in her eyes held a heated flame as she dropped the blanket from around her shoulders and waltzed up the steps.

A wry smile came over me beforeI jerked to my feet and followed her up the stairs while doing my best to avoid the steps that creaked.

Before I made it through the doorway to her bedroom, Aera jumped into my arms and captured my lips between hers.

"Are you sure you want to do this?"

"Positive," she moaned, claiming my lips once again. Only this time did I allow myself to drink in the sweetness of her kiss.

With a firm grip on the underside of her thighs, I walked us over to the bed and eased her down into my lap. Once settled, Aera instinctively ground herself against my length as her tongue teasingly danced against mine.

In one swift motion, I rolled us over so she was on her back, which gave me better leverage to work my hips between her legs. Our breaths grew heavy as each of our kisses held more heat than the last.

Warmth spread throughout my veins and my hands impatiently ached to explore more of her body. Gripping her waist, I skated one hand across the silken skin on her stomach before undoing her zipper. Aera helped by lifting her hips and wiggling down her pants until she laid before me in only her bra and thong.

I cupped her pussy and instantly felt her wetness through the thin material. My impatience grew explosive as I slipped a finger underneath the fabric at her waistline while simultaneously kissing down her body.

Shimmying her panties off, I licked up and down her center before sucking her clit between my lips. A shudder of pleasure erupted from her mouth, and her moans flooded the surrounding room.

I lined up two fingers with her opening and her body

welcomed me into her tight heat. It wasn't long before I curled them upward to that spongy spot that I knew would make her see stars.

As expected, her head flew back against the pillow and she let out eager cries for more. "Another finger, please," she begged against my lips, wriggling beneath me.

Obliging, I slipped my pointer finger inside, causing my pinkie to graze downward and brush her asshole. Aera looked up at me with widened eyes that quickly rolled back in her head as she inched closer to ecstasy.

A spat of lusty moans spilled from her lips as I tantalized her with my fingers. "Oh, my god. Oh, my god. I think I'm going to…"

I continued to flick my tongue against her clit, keeping the same motion so she didn't lose her orgasm as it rushed to the peak. Moments later, she cried out screams of pleasure as her body shook rigorously around my hand.

She looked like a vision when she came for me like that. And knowing I was the only person she'd ever finished with sent a primal surge of warmth straight to my cock.

I slowed my fingers as she rode out her first orgasm to give her a chance to catch her breath. "Do you want my cock this time?"

"Yes," she whimpered, pulling me up to taste her arousal on my lips while unbuttoning my jeans.

My dick jumped at her eagerness.

Throwing off my clothes, my cock sprung free, and a devilish smile grew on Aera's lips at the sight.

"Lie down," she commanded.

My lips broke into a mischievous grin as I followed her direction. Moments later, she wiggled her way on top of me and sank onto my cock, taking all of me at once.

A moan of pleasure expelled from my mouth as she found rhythm rotating her hips in slow circles around my length. She kept me on edge until she was ready to send us through the intoxicating peak of desire simultaneously.

I thought my hunger for this girl couldn't get worse, but when Aera fell into a sweaty, panting heap on top of me, wholeness radiated through my chest, which only multiplied my craving tenfold.

8

AERA

ONE MIGHT SAY I'd spent two full weeks in Comets Valley, but seeing as I could count on one hand the number of times Elliot and I had left the house in the past few days, that seemed like a bit of a stretch.

I might not have had the chance to explore all the town had to offer yet, but Elliot had done such a thorough job exploring my body that I didn't have enough brainpower to care.

"You know we have to leave this room, eventually." Elliot kissed the tip of my nose as I lay nuzzled between the warmth of his chest with the comforter draped over my back. "At least long enough to wash the sheets because it reeks of sex in here."

"Please don't tell me we have to re-drown everything in lavender."

A chuckle rumbled up from his throat, and a small smile drew up my lips.

In truth, when I came back to town the other day to grab my tablet, I hadn't planned on staying longer than a night. But Elliot's ploy to keep me in a continuous orgasm-induced coma, so I'd stay was working in both of our favors.

And as much as I enjoyed the highs he gave me; it was moments like this—when the heat between us had settled and our bodies were tangled comfortably between the sheets—that kept me staying day after day.

The chemistry between us wasn't forced or uncomfortable. In fact, it was the furthest from either of those things. Being with Elliot was easy, and the best part about it was that he made me forget the loneliness I'd grown to know so well back in Los Angeles.

"Maybe we could go into town later? I promised Calliope I'd stop by to see her before I leave again." I didn't miss Elliot's down-turned facial features at the last few words.

The last week we'd done our best to avoid discussions about me leaving for good. But seeing as I was leaving the day after tomorrow, we couldn't escape from the topic much longer.

I knew I couldn't stay here with him forever, but as the days sped by, I wondered what it would be like to bring Elliot back to LA with me. He came back to Comets Valley for a reason, but would he ever be interested in moving away from here again?

I tucked off the thought, reminding myself that this thing between us was just a fling. This time next month, both of us will probably have forgotten about each other entirely.

"We could go to the Christmas festival this afternoon if you want. Calliope has a booth every year, so we can drop by and see her then."

I sucked in a breath, sitting up in bed with widened eyes. This had to be *the* Christmas Eve festival Juliet mentioned was Comets Valley's claim to fame. She said the town rarely ever got tourists, but this was the biggest event of the year, and people traveled from all of the surrounding towns to take part in it.

This place was already everything I'd dreamed of and more, so it was hard for me to imagine seeing Main Street filled to the brim with people buying candied pecans and shopping for gifts at the display stands.

The thought alone was too perfect to be true.

"There'll be ice skating…" Elliot added in an attempt to convince me further. What he didn't know was that I'd made up my mind well before I arrived to town and we were sure as hell going to the festival.

"What time does it start?" I gently pecked along his jawline before placing a lingering kiss on his lips.

"We have a few hours to kill."

"Good." I smirked.

Keeping me tight against his chest, Elliot rolled me onto my back and settled his hips against my core. Both of us still naked from the last round, he slid his length across my sticky slit, igniting a new spark of arousal inside me.

A tingle of warmth spread outward from my center as he kissed down my neck before dipping lower to nip my taut peaks. I yelped with a laugh which quickly turned to cries of pleasure as he licked and massaged my swollen breasts until they were so sensitive I could've come from that alone.

One of my favorite things about Elliot was that he was so in tune with my body that he almost always knew whether or not I was getting off on what he was doing to me. Confidence exuded from him the entire time, and it made me want to melt all over him.

Not daring to break apart from my lips, he lined up

with my entrance and buried himself inside me on the first stroke. I arched my back as a whirl of heat swarmed throughout my body and settled into my core.

He filled me so deeply with every thrust I felt like I couldn't possibly take any more of what he had to give. Yet, I abandoned my thoughts and allowed myself to be whirled into the fullness of the sensations I was feeling.

"You look so pretty taking all of me like that," he rasped before quickly slipping out of me to grab one of the throw pillows that'd been kicked to the end of the bed. Lifting my hips, he shoved the pillow underneath. When he entered me again, the new angle made it feel like he was deeper inside me than he'd ever been before. And the stars clouding my vision were proof that was a possibility.

I was a panting, moaning mess who'd given up all efforts at trying to make myself look cute while I came. Because when I did, I knew I was going to explode into a thousand pieces, and there couldn't possibly be a way to look cute while doing that.

"Tell me how good it feels." The smug grin Elliot wore while he pounded in and out of my heat sent me spiraling into another dimension.

"I... can't think right now," I stammered between thrusts. "H-how do you expect me to f-formulate words?"

The grin on his face only got bigger and my non-response after must've been proof enough of how he made me feel, which for the record, was really fucking good.

I was almost thirty years old and all my prior sexual experiences had only been with one man—well, aside from the current fling I was taking part in—and all it took was one week with Elliot to show me what I'd missed out on for an entire decade.

Yet another reason to be angry at myself for staying

with Tye for so long. The guy didn't give me an orgasm for ten years— ten years!—and this one figured it out in less than twenty minutes.

What the hell was wrong with me?

"Come back to me, gorgeous."

See. That's what I meant. Tye would've never noticed nor cared if I was thinking myself out of an orgasm. Elliot just… knew. And instead of letting it get to his head, he used it as fuel to bring me back on course.

I groaned, unsure whether it was from pleasure or general frustration with myself. But probably pleasure based on the way Elliot was pounding into me with long, hard thrusts while his thumb circled my clit.

"Faster, please. I'm going to come."

Gripping my hips firmly with both hands, he picked up the pace of his strokes while I slid my hand down my torso to take over working my clit.

The sound of my wetness and our bodies slapping against each other resounded off the walls. And his groans… oh my god. Hearing him so unapologetically vocal made my pussy clench around his length even harder.

There was something about knowing he was enjoying this just as much as I was that sent a thrill of euphoria scorching through my veins.

"Come with me," he urged.

With our eyes locked, my throbbing core trembled around his cock as my climax took over, electrifying every nerve ending in my body. Mere seconds later, his release triggered, and I milked each drop of cum from his cock as he spurted inside me.

"So perfect," Elliot murmured, sighing in exhaustion as he rested his head on my heart.

"Ready to go again?" I asked, gasping for breath.

"You're insatiable, you know that?"

"Don't worry, it's okay if you can't keep up," I taunted, raking my fingertips through his dark, disheveled hair.

"I'll make time to punish you for that later, but let's get you some water first." He pushed himself up and pecked my lips before climbing out of bed and heading for the kitchen.

It was in that moment that I couldn't help but feel like this fling between us was much more than a way to relieve some sexual tension. All he did was step out of the room and my body ached for more of his touch. For more time together. For more of him.

I'd come to terms with only having two more days here. But what I hadn't worked out though, was how I was going to have the courage to leave Elliot behind at the end of this and go back to normal life like nothing happened between us.

THE COMETS VALLEY 42nd Annual Christmas Eve Festival was everything I'd imagined and then some. We filled our day with delicious snacks and live music from The Lunar Comets, the town's notorious band. Followed by another captivating evening, wrapped between the sheets for hours on end.

That night while I dozed off, I made the decision that I'd be coming back here next Christmas to do this all over again. I only hoped that Elliot would be game for a repeat of our sexcapades as well.

It had been days, if not weeks, since I thought about work and what awaited me back in Los Angeles. And now that it was my last day in Comets, the only thing I wanted was to forget about it all for a few more hours.

Elliot slipped a firm hand through my hair while he kissed me deep and slow. Sometime last night, we moved the Christmas tree from the living room and up to the bedroom. Now, the miniature bulbs were the only source of light illuminating the darkened room around us.

Somewhere along the way, the two of us had lost track of time, which was how we found ourselves wide awake at four in the morning. Our time together was coming to a close, and neither of us wanted to waste a moment sleeping.

Flames of passion burned between us as our tongues glided against each other. Elliot took his time while I savored every touch and committed it to memory.

We molded our bodies together in harmony, and our breaths grew heavier with each slow, drugging kiss. Caressing my lips, Elliot lined up with my entrance and inched his length inside me, and my back arched instinctively as pleasurable warmth spread outward from my core.

The fire between us fueled to new heights as we moved together, inching toward the edge of bliss as one. With our bodies fused together, my inner walls rippled around him at the same time, Elliot grunted from the satisfaction of his release.

After multiple mind-numbing orgasms, the two of us lay tangled between the sheets in a breathless bundle, unsure where his body started and mine ended. There was nothing I wanted more than to stay here with him like this forever.

Tranquil silence flowed between us as minutes passed until the first rays of sunlight surfaced through the blinds. Brushing my hair out of my eyes, Elliot's expression grew somber and his voice choked, "Stay."

Avoiding his eyes, a weary sigh expelled from my lungs. "You know I can't do that."

"Why don't we try long distance? I could get a place in LA and stay until I'm able to find a house here," he offered, so sure of himself. So confident the separation between us wouldn't be a burden on our relationship.

In all honesty, I wanted to keep seeing him and to believe we could make this work. But seeing as our lives were geographically in two completely different places the odds of us surviving the distance seemed improbable.

The way I saw it, once I got back to Los Angeles, my life would resume as normal. And if he came with me, eventually my long nights spent at the office would wear on him and crumble the passion between us. Then one day down the road, when he finally decided he had enough, he'd move on to someone else and I'd revert deeper into the shell of a person I was before meeting him.

It was almost as if the harder I tried to ignore the reality of our situation the last few weeks, the more it was coming back to hurt me in the end.

"And then what?" I queried. "What will we do once you move back to Comets Valley and I'm eleven hours away?"

"I'll fly down most weekends and when work isn't too heavy on your end, you can come up to visit again."

"So what, we're just going to do that every weekend until this eventually fizzles out?" His head reared back at my words and I wished I could've taken them back as quickly as they tumbled from my mouth. "Look, these last few weeks together have been… amazing. More than amazing, even. But I just don't see how we could make this work long term."

"Would you change your mind if I told you I was in love with you?"

I tensed, staring at him blankly. My cynical inner voice cut through my thoughts, convincing me his words were false. That he couldn't possibly have fallen for me in such a short amount of time.

"Aera?"

"I—I'm… processing." A long moment passed without words. Gathering my thoughts, I sucked in a steadying breath before speaking again. "Elliot… I think that maybe we should let the time we spent together be just that—a perfect memory to look back on—instead of tainting it with the possibility of something we can't predict the outcome of."

My heart sunk to the pit of my stomach when I saw the pained look in his eyes. Tightness constricted my throat as I croaked out a teary-eyed apology.

"It's fine. No, really, it's fine. You told me from the start what you wanted, and I shouldn't have held the hope that you'd change your mind." His words were understanding yet held a blatant sting.

"Maybe… if I come back next year, we could do this again?" I offered as he pulled back the sheets and slipped out of bed.

"Sure," he replied curtly, picking up his jeans off the ground and throwing them on. "I should really go home and get some sleep before my, uh, meeting later."

That was a lie, and both of us knew it.

I nodded, dragging my gaze down to the sheets.

I will not cry. I will not cry.

I silently begged for him to crawl back into bed and take hold of my lips long enough to ease the gnawing ache in my chest, though I knew doing so would only make that ache remarkably worse.

"Have a safe drive back," he mumbled so low I hardly registered his words.

I flickered my gaze upward to give him a sheepish smile, but by the time I did, he was gone.

It was only once I heard the last of his heavy footsteps echo off the walls and the crack of the front door closing that I allowed the extraordinary void that burned inside my chest to consume me.

I'd come to terms with only having a few more hours here, but what I hadn't planned for was Elliot leaving me behind at the end of this like nothing happened between us.

9

ELLIOT

APPROXIMATELY TWELVE SECONDS after walking out the front door, I regretted it.

By the time I made it to the front porch of my parents' house, I was seriously contemplating turning on my heels and jogging back to Juliet's place. I wanted to barge through the door, take Aera into my arms, and offer her whatever she wanted as long as it meant she'd stay.

But knowing Aera, I'd place my bets that she'd already packed her suitcases into the back seat of her car by now.

Ignoring the below-freezing temperature, I plopped down onto one of the red rocking chairs and analyzed all the ways that I went wrong. For starters, there was the part where I walked out instead of having a conversation like a grown fucking man.

I hung my head in my hands and let out a frustrated groan. Only, I wasn't upset with Aera. If there was anyone to be aggravated with, it was myself.

Her words hurt me more than I liked to admit. The magnetism I felt between us wasn't something that I ever envisioned "fizzling out"—her words, not mine—between us. And instead of talking through my feelings like a logical human being, I allowed the weight of her words to punch me straight in the gut.

Though in retrospect, her words weren't what hurt me the most, instead it was the fact that she was willing to give up on us so easily. Prematurely dooming us before giving us the chance to try.

Feeling drained, I rose from the rocking chair and ran my hands down my cheeks before grabbing the key I knew would be under the mat and wandering inside.

"Elliot, is that you?" Mom's muffled voice sounded from the kitchen.

"It's me."

"Honey, Elliot's back!" she called over to my dad in the living room, who was too captivated with reading the newspaper in his recliner to respond with more than a grunt. "Hi sweetheart, where have you been?"

Walking into the room, she came over to give me a warm welcome. "I've been staying with a friend for a while."

"And by friend, you mean the pretty girl who was staying in Juliet's place?" Mom quirked a brow at me before walking over to the coffeepot and holding it up in offering. I nodded a quick approval.

I should've known word would've gotten around town about the two of us. Especially after Aera's partial strip tease at Sal's. I'd pay a couple grand to go back in time and see the look on the faces of the older ladies who met for coffee at Steamy Beans every morning to exchange meaningless information about other townspeople.

Then there was the other afternoon where I'd unapologetically paraded around town with her latched to my side during the festival. The last time the people of Comets

Valley had seen me on a date was my senior prom, half a lifetime ago. I should've suspected bringing a woman around for the first time in nearly two decades would generate a significant amount of buzz.

"Yeah," I sighed. "Although, after the morning I just had, I'm not entirely sure we'd be considered friends anymore."

"That bad?" She pursed her lips, handing me over a mug that was much less decorative than those in the cupboard at my sister's house.

"And this girl… you like her?"

"I think it's safe to say that I more than like her."

She hummed, leaning back against the edge of the counter, "Did your father ever tell you about our first date?"

"Yeah… the two of you met for dinner on a Friday night, but neither of you wanted to go home, so you stayed out until Sunday evening when you had no choice but to go back."

"Yup," she said with a reminiscent smile. "I bet he didn't tell you about the part about me breaking his heart at the end of our date though, did he?"

"What?" My mouth went slack-jawed. That was news to me.

She nodded. "When he dropped me off at my apartment Sunday evening, I expected him to walk me to the front door and tell me he wanted to do this same thing again the next weekend. You could see why I was caught off guard when instead of asking me on another date, he asked me to move in with him…"

I lifted a brow, urging her to continue.

"We'd known each other for forty-eight hours, yet he knew he wanted to make a life together." She took a long sip from her mug. "It terrified me, so I told him I'd call him, but I didn't. Not until the next Friday when I went on a date with Gill Mullins and realized I made a mistake."

"How'd you get him back?"

"That was the simple part." She smirked. My father glanced up from his article and gave her a knowing smile. "I lied and told Gill I was going to the restroom, but instead, I went to the kitchen and asked to borrow their phone. Your dad picked me up from the restaurant fifteen minutes later, and… well, you know the rest."

The thought of Aera going on a date with another man back in Los Angeles made a twinge of jealousy spark in my chest.

"What I'm getting at here is that if she's the one for you, she'll find her way back. Just give her some time."

Taking a deep breath, I replayed the last few weeks in my head with my mom's words at the forefront of my brain.

Just give her some time.

"I have to change first, but I'm going to head back to Juliet's and wait until she gets home."

"Be sure to give Mr. Whiskers our love." Setting her mug in the sink, Mom placed a gentle hand on my shoulder before sauntering into the living room and curling up in the chair with my father.

BACK AT JULIET'S, my breath caught in my lungs when I walked into her kitchen to find a takeout napkin with

Aera's phone number scribbled on it. But it was the small heart under her name that did me in.

A number of emotions as I fell back onto the couch and opened my phone to plug her into my contacts. If I called her now, would she answer? More importantly, if she did, what would I say when she picked up?

"What do you say, Mr. Whiskers? Do we call her or let it be?" I tilted my head in question at the orange tabby sitting next to me. Ignoring me, he hopped off the couch and staggered away.

I take it that was his version of a no?

A few minutes passed of me staring at Aera's name with my thumb hovering over the "call" button when a frantic cluster of knocks sounding at the door startled me.

Throwing my phone onto the couch beside me, I rose to my feet and walked over to the front door, where the frenzied knocking had yet to cease.

Jesus, the only person who would be this immodest with their household etiquette would be my sister.

Grasping the doorknob, I whipped open the door. "Juliet, seriously. Did you forget how to use your ke—"

Only the woman on my doorstep wasn't my sister.

Instead, the most breathtaking woman I'd ever seen with her jet-black hair and the darkest brown eyes, was staring up at me with labored breaths.

"You're not my sister." Shock coated my voice as I swept my eyes over the woman standing before me.

She was here. She came back.

"My flight got canceled."

"You drove."

"I know," she panted, and the corners of her lips curled upward. Unbridled anticipation roared so vigorously in the space between us I could hardly process what was happening.

"Tell me you didn't come back for only your tablet this time."

"No." She shook her head with a laugh, taking a step closer to me. "I was actually thinking that maybe you could use a date, you know, to Sal's for New Year's Eve…"

I took a step closer to her and tucked a rogue piece of hair behind her ear.

"You're sure about this?"

She nodded. "I don't know the logistics… or how we'll fit into each other's lives, but I know that I love you." Aera cut the final inches of distance between us by diving into my arms in one swift movement. "And I think that's as good of a reason as any to—"

I cut her off, searing our lips together in an unbreakable, possessive kiss. It was then that I vowed to myself, if a day came where she doubted my love for her again, then I'd give her as much time as she needed to find her way back to me.

EPILOGUE

Aera
One year later

"WE'RE GOING TO BE LATE!" Elliot called up the stairs to the master bedroom, where I sat at my vanity, brushing on a final stroke of eyeshadow for good measure.

After a year of back and forth between Los Angeles and Comets, we spent the entire month of December christening as many rooms as possible in our freshly renovated home. Which was conveniently located on the same street as Juliet's cottage.

Whenever we came back to town, it felt like we'd never left. This place was our break away from the chaos of city life and where our best memories from the last year had been made.

"Aera, seriously. We're officially late!"

"Fashionably late, I hope?" I shot him a wink, waltzing

down the steps in a gold ball gown I'd designed especially for this event.

"That's an awful joke… every time you make it." Taking my hand in his, Elliot placed a gentle kiss against the back of it, which made my heart somersault in my chest.

"You're telling me it hasn't grown on you even a little bit yet?"

"Not the slightest." With a smirk on his lips, he placed a gentle kiss against my temple. "You ready?"

"As ready as I'll ever be."

The only event better than the Comets Valley Christmas Eve Festival was Sal's New Year's Bash. Last year—no thanks to my then boyfriend—I was severely under dressed, so in typical fashion, I had no choice but to be best dressed this year.

It wasn't a competition, but I was making it one for my own personal enjoyment.

Before walking out the door, Elliot wrapped my faux fur coat over my shoulders. And with his arm wrapped securely around me, we ambled through the still decorated streets taking time to admire our neighbor's holiday cheer despite the chill that was settling into the depths of my bones.

Minutes later, a familiar bell I'd grown to know well over the last year chimed as Elliot swung open the door to Sal's. Music exploded from the sound system and a crowd like I'd never seen before filled the room to max capacity.

Most surprising of all, every square inch of this place had been stripped of the Christmas decor and replaced with black and gold streamers strung across the ceiling, and matching balloons covered the floor.

Elliot rested a hand on my lower back as he showed

our tickets to the bouncer—and by bouncer, I meant some high school kid dressed in a rented tux—at the entrance before leading us deeper into the room. Before we made it twenty steps inside, the bubbliest blonde I'd ever met plowed through swarms of people and dashed toward us with outstretched arms.

The one thing I loved most about Juliet was that, without fail, she was always the most vibrant person in the room. Even as she made her way over to Elliot and me, people's gazes were instantly drawn to her allure.

"You guys are just in time!" she squealed with delight, throwing her hands around both of our necks at once like we hadn't all seen each other at Christmas dinner last week.

I shot Elliot a smug glare. *"We're late,"* my ass.

"Actually, we have news to share with you…" I started.

"No way, I've got some news to share with you guys too!" Juliet's entire face spread into a smile. "You guys go first."

"We're engaged."

"You're what?" she exclaimed, bouncing her eyes between the two of us. Elliot and I shot each other a wide grinned glance.

I held out my left hand, and her eyes grew large at the emerald-cut diamond on my finger.

"And we're moving to the Malibu house full time," Elliot finished the rest of our news for me, and this time Juliet's mouth fell open.

On Christmas morning, not only was I surprised that Elliot dropped down on one knee but also that his proposal was quickly followed up by the admission that he wanted to venture back into the real estate realm and Malibu seemed like the best place.

"This really makes my news about giving away half my mug collection sound really lame." Juliet made a face, and Elliot and I both barked out a laugh.

Overhearing the news, Elliot's friend, Gabe, strolled over to give his congratulations. While they caught up, Juliet and I grabbed seats at a tabletop that opened up next to us.

"Who would've guessed both of us falling for that stupid home swapping advertisement would've led to all this?"

"Crazy, isn't it?" I reflected on it with a small laugh. "Speaking of which, has Ben called yet?"

"Nope." She shrunk down into her chair a bit.

"Don't stress, he'll call. I know he will."

As if the universe had been listening, her phone buzzed, and when she flashed the screen toward me, Ben's name was in capital letters at the top of the screen.

She threw back the rest of the champagne in her flute and slipped out of her seat. "Umm, I'm gonna…"

"Go," I insisted with a grin so wide it made my cheeks ache.

I danced my gaze around the room, taking in the people and place I'd grown to adore so deeply. While I knew moving to Malibu was the right choice for now, a substantial part of me knew we'd be back to make this place our forever home one day.

"I heard the news, congratulations!" Calliope beamed up at me, coming out of nowhere. Damn, somehow I always forgot how quickly news traveled around here. "Not to downplay your moment, but guess who's ready to cash in that job offer?"

I gasped, "Really?"

She nodded and her face split into a wide grin.

"Thank god, because I'm going to be taking quite a bit of time off soon, and you're the only person I trust as my replacement." I squeezed her close before perking up. "Oh, and you can stay in my condo!"

"What are you guys going to do with your house here?"

"Elliot wants us to rent it out. Something about wanting more people to experience the magic of this place… you know how sentimental he gets."

"Two minutes!" A jovial male voice bellowed through the bar.

"Go find your man. I'll come by the house before you guys leave again, and we can talk logistics." She pulled me in for one last quick hug before disappearing between the masses almost as quickly as she arrived.

Scanning through the sea of partygoers, my eyes caught on a handsome man across the room. A smile flung free from my lips, and anticipation felt like a shot buzzing through my veins as I crossed the room and settled into the warmth of his arms.

"I was hoping you'd find your way back to me." Elliot quipped, tugging me closer to his chest.

"Always."

Zealous excitement coursed through the room as everyone counted down in unison, "Three! Two! One… Happy New Year!"

"Happy New Year, gorgeous." His smile eased wide as he bent down to claim my lips with a passionate kiss.

"Happy New Year, Dad," I whispered against his lips.

It took half a second for the recognition of my words to flood across his face. A flurry of emotions flickered through his eyes all at once until he softened his gaze at me and placed a gentle hand on my stomach.

I was the furthest thing from an expert at life, but I knew one thing to be true. When the universe laid an opportunity in your lap—creepily curated ad and all—it was worth the taking.

Who knows, maybe it'll be the best damn thing that's ever happened to you.

The End.

CHECK OUT AERA'S BROTHER AND
SISTER-IN-LAW'S BOOK THE
FANTASY LEAGUE AVAILABLE NOW.

MORE BY MEG

The League

Scarlett & Abel - The Fantasy League

Mae & October - The Red Zone

Lea & Fortune - The Silent Count

Christmas Vacation Novellas

Aera & Elliot - Christmas in Comets Valley

Juliet & Peter - Merry in Malibu

Banks Brothers

Lyla & Barrett - The Physical Attraction Seminar

ACKNOWLEDGMENTS

Zoe, for being so wonderful to work with and giving me invaluable feedback.

My Brother's Editor, you've done it again, and I love you for it. Endless thank you's.

Roxana, for combing through this with a fresh set of eyes.

Melody, for illustrating and designing the most beautiful cover I could have imagined. Let's do this a million more times, yeah?

Finally, to my readers, who have already changed my life in more ways than I ever dreamed possible. I know I've said it once before, but I'll say it again for good measure. There isn't enough thank you's in the world to express my gratitude for each of you. I'm beyond thankful!

ABOUT THE AUTHOR

Meg Reading is a contemporary romance author whose family knew she was destined to become a writer long before she did. Although, her imaginary friends and the stack of fictional stories she wrote about her middle school crushes made it kind of obvious. However, Meg was too engulfed in reading books to notice her calling, and it took her another decade to finally put down the books and start writing her own instead.

She is a self-proclaimed homebody who has two cats named Gomez and Fester. When she's not reading, writing, or procrastinating, you can find her incessantly re-watching Gilmore Girls and surviving off of copious amounts of hazelnut coffee.

Website: www.megreading.com
Newsletter: www.megreading.com/newsletter

amazon.com/author/megreading

tiktok.com/@megreading

instagram.com/megreading

pinterest.com/megreadingauthor

Printed in Great Britain
by Amazon

10598083R00068